She Should Not Be Allowing Tariq To Kiss Her Like This.

Tariq needed a wife who would do her duty...and that woman was not her. So what on earth was she doing responding to her soon-to-be-ex like this?

She tore out of his arms and put half the length of the room between them. "I don't want this."

"Liar." His voice was flat, his face expressionless. The light in his golden eyes had been extinguished. "You responded to me."

He was right. But she couldn't afford to let him know that. "Maybe I'd have responded to any attractive man."

"Any man?" It was a soft snarl, dangerous. "Like the one waiting back for you in Auckland?"

Jayne's heart thumped in her chest, so loudly she feared he might hear. "Your lack of trust is the reason why I don't want to be married to you anymore."

"Do you blame me?" His mouth tightened. "No, don't answer that. Our marriage is over. In a month you will have your divorce."

Dear Reader,

I found it very hard to write this letter—mostly because I've reached the end of the BILLIONAIRE HEIRS trilogy about cousins Zac, Angelo and Tariq. And I don't really want to say goodbye to these gorgeous men. Not yet. Nor do I want to say goodbye to Pandora, Gemma and Jayne. I've spent so much time with these people over the past months that they've become a part of my life.

But now it's time to go out and meet—even embrace☺—new characters. Learn about them. What they like. What they loathe. And most importantly what happens to them when they fall in love…

Because at the heart of it all it's fabulous to create people who, after a rocky beginning, end up falling in love—and convincing readers that their love will last a lifetime. And sometimes, like Jayne and Tariq, they don't get it right the first time around. In *The Desert Bride of Al Zayed* Jayne and Tariq have a second chance at love…and a chance to get it right.

Take care,

Tessa

PS: Don't forget that you can find out more about my upcoming releases, over at www.tessaradley.com. Please come and visit!

TESSA RADLEY

THE DESERT BRIDE OF AL ZAYED

Published by Silhouette Books

America's Publisher of Contemporary Romance

SILHOUETTE BOOKS

ISBN-13: 978-0-373-76835-6
ISBN-10: 0-373-76835-4

THE DESERT BRIDE OF AL ZAYED

Copyright © 2007 by Tessa Radley

Books by Tessa Radley

Silhouette Desire

Black Widow Bride #1794
Rich Man's Revenge #1806
*The Kyriakos Virgin Bride #1822
*The Apollonides Mistress Scandal #1829
*The Desert Bride of Al Zayed #1835

*Billionaire Heirs

TESSA RADLEY

loves traveling, reading and watching the world around her. As a teen Tessa wanted to be an intrepid foreign correspondent. But after completing a bachelor of arts and marrying her sweetheart, she became fascinated with law and ended up studying further and becoming an attorney in a city practice.

A six-month break traveling through Australia with her family re-awoke the yen to write. And life as a writer suits her perfectly; traveling and reading count as research and as for analyzing the world...well, she can think *what if* all day long. When she's not reading, traveling or thinking about writing, she's spending time with her husband, her two sons—or her zany and wonderful friends. You can contact Tessa through her Web site www.tessaradley.com.

I grew up surrounded by inspiring women.
My mother, Ria, who always stays true to herself.
As well as Sophie and Esme who give so generously of
themselves. Thank you all for your love.

Much thanks to Melissa Jeglinski and Karen Solem
for giving me the freedom to write.

And Abby Gaines, Karina Bliss and Sandra Hyatt—
thank you for never being farther than a call away!

One

"I want a divorce."

The moment she'd blurted the words out, Jayne felt her pulse quicken. She squeezed her eyes shut…and waited. The silence on the other end of the line was absolute.

"No."

The answer rang with finality over the vast distance that separated Zayed from New Zealand. Tariq's voice was smooth and deep and very, very cool. Like ice. Tingling shivers of apprehension started to dance along Jayne's spine. She recognised that sensation. It meant trouble.

Jayne gripped the handset until her fingers hurt. "But we've been separated for over five years. I thought you'd be jumping for joy at the prospect of a divorce." *And your father, too.* She refrained from adding the dig. Mention of his father, the Emir of Zayed, tended to result in arguments—she'd learned that a long time ago. And she didn't want a battle with no ceasefire in sight, she simply wanted a divorce.

But this was not going quite as she'd planned. From the outset Jayne had intended avoiding any direct contact with Tariq—or his father. She'd phoned the Emir's chief aide, Hadi al Ebrahim, and had bluntly stated that more than five years had passed since Tariq had banished her from Zayed. Tariq was a citizen of Zayed and their marriage had been conducted in accordance with the laws of his country. According to the laws of Zayed, parties had to be separated for five years before a divorce could be petitioned.

The legal waiting time was over. She wanted to set divorce proceedings in motion. The excruciatingly polite aide had taken her number and promised to call her back.

But the aide's promised call hadn't come. Instead Sheikh Tariq bin Rashid al Zayed, her husband—no, her hopefully soon-to-be-ex-husband—had called.

Only to refuse her request.

No. No explanation. No softening the blow. Just a very blunt, very final *"No."*

Jayne resisted the urge to stamp her foot. Instead she tried for her most reasonable teacher's voice, and said, "You haven't seen me for years, Tariq. Don't you think it's time for us both to move on?" From a past that had brought her more pain and anguish than she'd ever anticipated.

"It's not yet time."

Jayne's heart skipped a beat. She sensed all her well-laid plans to start a new degree with the new year, to start dating again, to come out of hibernation and start living a life, unravelling. "Not time? What do you mean it's not yet time? Of course it's time. All you need to do is sign—"

"Come to Zayed and we'll talk about it, Jayne."

Even over the distance between them the husky sound of her very ordinary name on his tongue sounded sensual and intimate and had the power to make her shiver. It was madness.

"I don't want to talk. I just want a divorce." Jayne heard the touch of shrillness in her voice. She could see her brand-new life, her well-laid plans going up in smoke. Damn Tariq.

"Why?" His voice changed, became harsh and abrupt. "Why are you suddenly so desperate for a divorce, my faithless woman? Is there finally a man who objects to having a woman with a husband?"

A brief hesitation. She thought about Neil, the nice accountant her brother-in-law had introduced her to three months ago. He'd asked her out, but she hadn't accepted. Yet. "No! You've got it all—"

"We will meet in Zayed," her husband decreed. "There will be no divorce. Not yet. But it is possible that the time will come soon. Very soon. We will talk."

"Tariq—"

But he was already firing information about dates and flights and visas at her. Belatedly Jayne realised that she no longer held her Zayedi passport, she'd left it behind in the bedroom she'd shared with Tariq on that terrible last day. She'd had no intention of ever returning. She'd have to apply for a visa to go to Zayed, which meant at least a week of delay.

"Tariq." It was a desperate call.

He paused and the sudden silence that stretched between them was shattering.

Jayne swallowed, her mouth dry. Then, more quietly, she said, "Can't we meet somewhere—" *neutral* "—else?" Tariq would not come to New Zealand; it was too far. He was a busy man. And she didn't want him here, destroying her safe haven.

But there had to be other options. Somewhere where she wouldn't need to revisit those traumatic weeks before the end of their marriage, somewhere she wouldn't have to walk through the corridors of the lavish palace that had stifled her dreams, or confront the two men who had killed her soul. "What about London?"

"There are…problems…in Zayed. I cannot leave."

She thought about that for a long moment. "I *can't* come to Zayed," she said at last.

"Can't or won't?"

She didn't answer.

"Then let me make it easy for you. If you don't come to Zayed, Jayne, I will oppose any application you make for a divorce."

The words were chilling, even though the tone that delivered them was rich and lingering. The laws of Zayed stated that no divorce could be granted unless the husband consented. As much as it riled her, she needed Tariq's consent.

Unless she went to Zayed, Tariq would deny her the one thing she wanted above all else: her freedom.

"Don't forget to send me photos of Zayed."

Jayne had almost reached the front door of her sister's house, the Louis Vuitton bag clutched in her hand, when the request caused her to pause. She turned to look at the three people gathered in a huddle to see her off, the three people she loved most in the world—her sister and her two nieces. Raising an eyebrow at her elder niece, Jayne asked, "What kind of photos?"

"Of the desert…the palace—anything cool."

"It's very hot in the desert, not cool at all. Certainly not as cool as anything here in Auckland." Jayne kept a straight face as she referred to her older niece's active social life, then broke into a smile when Samantha poked a pink tongue out. "What do you want the photos for?"

Samantha moved closer. "I'm doing a PowerPoint project on Zayed. Most of my class has never heard of it."

"I'm sure I can dig up some really up-to-date information while I'm there," Jayne promised, setting the heavy bag down for a moment and flexing her fingers. Samantha flashed a pleased grin and Jayne restrained herself from rumpling her niece's sleekly gelled hair. The style was so much more so-phisticated than the ponytail Samantha had worn last year. It was hard to believe that in less than a month Samantha would turn thirteen. A teenager.

"Great." Samantha beamed. "If I can wow my teacher, I might even get an A."

"Do you really have to go?"

A small hand tugged at her arm. Jayne looked down into the hazel eyes of her younger niece—her goddaughter—and her heart twisted.

"I really have to go, Amy, my sweet."

"Why?"

Jayne hesitated. *Why?* She thought of the abortive conver-sation with Tariq. How to even start to explain? "Because…" Her voice trailed away.

"'Because' is not an answer," Amy replied, her freckled face solemn.

"Quite frankly, I can't understand why you're going, either," Helen chipped in with typical older-sister impatience.

"After everything that happened in that godforsaken country, what Tariq and his horrid father did to you, why on earth would you contemplate going back?"

Jayne recognised her sister's impatience for what it was—concern. "Because I want a divorce—and it looks like going to Zayed is the only way I can get it."

Tariq had made that clear enough.

"Why Zayed?" Helen asked, her lips tight. "Why couldn't you have met in London?"

"It wasn't an option I was given." Jayne shrugged her shoulders. "That's Tariq. His way. Or no way."

"Are you sure he isn't up to something?" Helen fretted. "I don't trust him one bit."

"Hush, don't work yourself up." Jayne moved closer to her sister. Helen had never understood the attraction, the fascination that Tariq had held right from the moment that Jayne had walked into him in the Tate Gallery in London and landed ignominiously at his feet. How could she explain the untamed attraction Tariq had held? "There's no reason to be suspicious. Tariq wouldn't take me back if I came coated in twenty-four carat gold."

Helen's eyes sparked with indignation. In a low voice she murmured so that only Jayne could hear, "He never deserved you."

Emotion surged through Jayne. She slung an arm around her sister's shoulder and pulled her close. Helen smelled of talc and roses and the familiar comfort of home. "Thank you. And thank you for all the support you've given me. For everything."

"I don't want to see you in that state again." Helen hugged her back fiercely. "Five and a half years ago you were a mess."

"It won't happen again," Jayne vowed, suppressing the

sudden stab of apprehension. "I'm no longer nineteen. I'm older now, able to take care of myself."

"Famous last words. And it better not happen again, because this time I'll tell Tariq what a—" Helen cast a glance at the girls and lowered her voice "—*jerk* he is."

Her sister sounded so ferocious that Jayne couldn't help the giggle that escaped her. For the first time in a week, the tension that had been winding up in her chest subsided. Her sister would always be there for her. Family. Sisters. A sacred bond.

"I suggest you don't say that to Tariq's face." Just the thought of his freezing expression, the way he would look coldly down his elegant bladed nose, was enough to make Jayne chuckle again.

"You won't be here for my first day of school." Amy's desolate wail cut into Jayne's moment of good humour. Instantly all laughter dried up. Bending down, she swept Amy up until the little girl's eyes were level with hers.

"But I'll be thinking of you," Jayne promised. "I'll even know where you'll be sitting. Remember? You, mom and I went together to check your new school out?"

"I s'pose," Amy said reflectively. "And I'll have the pencils you bought me." She already sounded more cheerful. Jayne smiled at her sister over Amy's head, her throat tight.

A hoot sounded.

"Daddy's ready." Amy wriggled out of Jayne's arms.

Helen rushed over and then Jayne was wrapped in her sister's warm arms. "Take care, Jayne."

"I will." Jayne held on for a moment. A kiss on her sister's cheek and then she freed herself and picked up her bag. "I'd better not keep Nigel waiting. Look after yourself—and the

girls. I'll e-mail photos, I promise," she called to Helen and
Samantha as she hurried out the door. From beside the car,
Jayne gave them a last wave before getting into the idling car
where her brother-in-law waited to take her to the airport.

Finally Jayne let herself admit she wasn't looking forward
to the long flight that lay ahead. And she dreaded the coming
confrontation with the man who waited for her at the journey's
end.

The chilly air-conditioning in the international airport at
Jazirah, the capital of Zayed, took the edge off the searing heat
that shimmered over the runways outside the terminal
building. A deferential official took charge of Jayne the
instant she presented her passport and whisked her through
customs. He retrieved her luggage and showed her to a plush
seat in a sheltered alcove off the arrivals concourse, murmuring that he'd be back shortly.

Jayne attempted to assure him that she was quite capable
of organising her own transport, but he grew increasingly
agitated. He was obviously concerned by the fact that she was
travelling alone. Zayedi men could be extremely protective,
to the point of being overbearing. So Jayne subsided with a
shrug and watched him scurry away.

Pulling the white chiffon scarf out the side pocket of her
handbag where she'd tucked it in before leaving Auckland,
Jayne looped it around her neck. It wasn't a *hijab*, but it
would do. Zayed was more modern than its neighbouring
states, some of the youth even wore jeans, but most women
still adopted conservative dress. Jayne knew that the narrow
black trousers and casual geometric patterns of the black and
white shift dress she wore over them were acceptably

modest…even if they were straight out of this season's budget fashions in Auckland, a far cry from the traditional jilbab and colourful kaftans so many older married Zayedi women wore.

From where she sat, Jayne could see the long wall of glass that separated the airport from the drop-off zone outside. A fleet of shiny black Mercedeses were parked there, reminding her of the extent of the wealth in this desert sheikhdom.

A commotion a way down the concourse attracted her attention. Jayne rose to her feet to get a better look. A knot of uniformed men were causing a stir. Her gaze narrowed. She recognized those uniforms, they belonged to the Emir of Zayed's palace guard. They held some very unpleasant associations. The last time she'd seen the red and khaki colours had been here, at this airport, when the men wearing them had been charged with making sure she left Zayed.

Behind them she caught a glimpse of a tall man in a dark suit. His sheer imposing height and the familiar tilt of his head caused her heart to leap. *Tariq.* Jayne froze, her muscles tight, and her head swam with the sudden light-headedness caused by the panic that swirled through her.

He was coming closer. Her pulse grew choppy, loud in her ears. His head turned and their eyes connected. The first thing that struck her was that his eyes were still the colour of pure, molten gold. The second was that they were not the least bit welcoming.

Tariq raked her from head to toe, and his lip curled. Instantly all the old insecurities crashed back. She was plain Jayne Jones, in the everyday chain-store shift dress that she'd worn over her most comfortable black trousers for the flight.

The antipathy directed at her caused Jayne to stumble backward. Nothing had changed. Her husband detested her.

The earth rocked under her feet and she glanced away, disconcerted. And caught sight of the red carpet. Of the trio of little girls holding posies. But it took the black print on the brightly coloured banner two women were unfurling to jolt her into disbelief. Welcome Back Sheikhah, it read.

This dog-and-pony show was intended for her.

In a flash the reason for the official's agitation became clear. Her first meeting with Tariq was going to be conducted under public scrutiny. Jayne's palms grew clammy and her pulse started to race.

No.

She gave the gathering crowd a wild glance, took in the scaffolding with the mounted television cameras, clearly here to film her return. She was so not prepared for this hullabaloo. She'd come to meet Tariq, to talk in private about their divorce.

Tariq was walking with purpose. Backed by the squad of the palace guard, he looked dangerous, resolute. But Jayne knew that whatever the reason he'd demanded her return to Zayed, it had nothing to do with the love they had once shared.

She cast a frantic gaze around. People were milling forward, crowding around the red carpet, the guards and the powerful, commanding man in the heart of all the fuss. No, she hadn't come to be part of this…circus.

She wanted to meet Tariq on her terms. In private. Without an audience.

Two cameramen with huge cameras mounted on their shoulders that sported the local TV network logo rushed ahead of Tariq to capture the moment for the news. They blocked Tariq from her view.

Cautiously Jayne edged forward. No one was looking in her direction. With a surreptitious movement, she hitched the sheer scarf off her shoulders and draped it across her hair, then hoisted up the Louis Vuitton bag, a legacy from her past life with Tariq. Keeping her head down, she made quickly for the double sliding doors that led out of the airport. They hissed open and she escaped through.

The heat hit her like a wall. Oppressive. An inferno compared to the coolness in the airport and the temperate weather she'd left behind in Auckland. Jayne thought she heard a shout. She didn't look back. Instead she kept her head down and increased her pace. A taxi was parked behind the string of Mercedeses.

As she broke into a run a taxi driver straightened from the low railing he'd been leaning against and parted his lips into a smile that revealed stained yellow teeth separated with chunks of gold. "Taxi?" He opened the rear door and music blared out.

"Yes," she gasped, deafened as she fell into the backseat. When she didn't bother to haggle over the rate, his smile grew wider still. "Take me to the palace. Please."

The smile withered and he shot her a lightning-fast once-over glance, before climbing into the driver's seat and turning the radio down a notch.

"Hurry," she said, peering anxiously out the window beside her.

The motor roared, drowning out the radio for a moment, and her unsuspecting rescuer swerved out onto the strip of concrete road.

Driven by an impulse she could not explain, Jayne turned back to stare through the rear window at the glass doors through which she'd escaped.

His tie flapping with his stride, Tariq strode through the glass doors. Behind him followed the pack of palace guards. Jayne shrank back into her seat. Even from this distance she could tell that Tariq did not look pleased. The angle of his broad shoulders, the set of his head, the impatience in his long stride all showed his fury.

Trepidation coursed through her. This was no longer the young man she'd fallen in love with. This was a different Tariq. Older. Regal. The only son of the Emir of Zayed. A man accustomed to having his orders obeyed.

Jayne closed her eyes in relief at having gotten away. The taxi rocked from side to side as the driver darted through the traffic. Afraid that the roller-coaster motion might make her queasy, Jayne opened her eyes.

"Hey, slow down."

Jayne sighed in exasperation when her demand met no response, and leaned back into her seat to brace herself for the ride.

The airport was located a distance away from the city. On the left side of the car, the stony desert stretched away as far as the eye could see. On the other side, a narrow strip of land separated the six-lane highway from the azure sea. A couple of minutes later they passed the desalination plant that Jayne knew had cost millions to set up ten years ago.

The taxi driver swerved past a tourist camper van and cut across to the exit. Once away from the highway, they wove through the city streets between old historic buildings and modern glass skyscrapers.

"Are we being followed?" Clutching at the seat belt as they hurtled through an older section of the city between ancient mosques and colourful *souqs,* Jayne voiced her worst fear.

But the taxi driver didn't answer. Could he even hear her with the radio blaring? Jayne wished she'd sat up front. But this was Zayed, not New Zealand. Women didn't sit up front. Not unless they wanted the taxi driver to construe the move as flirtation. While Zayed was a safe country, a woman travelling alone had to take care not to attract unwelcome attention. She shouted the question more loudly.

The taxi driver glanced in the rear mirror. "No one is following."

But Jayne's apprehension didn't ease and the knot in her stomach grew tighter. Tariq was going to be fit to be tied. She shivered, then reason set in.

It was his own fault. He should have warned her. He should never have sprung that spectacle back at the airport on her. She gave her casual outfit a quick once-over. At least then she would've had the chance to dress up a little. Make the best of the little she had. Not that clothes and a little bit of makeup could bridge the gulf between them. They were too far apart. In every way.

She tried to set the worry aside, tried to tell herself that the sooner she met with Tariq in private and got it over with the better. But even that didn't help. Jayne's fingernails bit into her palms. She'd explain. She'd tell him that—

The sudden swerve of the taxi threw Jayne against the door, and she gave a shriek of fright. The driver leapt out of the car and Jayne could hear shouting.

When she emerged from the back of the car, her heart pounding, a shocking sight met her eyes. A youth was sprawled on the road, his bicycle lying on its side. He was groaning.

"Oh, my heavens." Jayne moved toward the victim but the taxi driver grabbed her arm.

"Wait, it could be a set-up…"

"How can it be a set-up? He's hurt!"

The youth was screaming now. A basket, its lid off, lay on the road and a clutch of ginger chickens were clucking in terror.

"Is he okay?" Jayne's first concern was for the youngster. "Did we hit him?"

"No, no. The idiot—"

The youth interrupted with a deluge in Arabic. Jayne held up her hand. "Is he hurt?"

The taxi driver rattled off and the boy muttered, shaking his head. Relieved Jayne said, "What about his bike?"

"No problem."

A crowd had started to gather. Quickly Jayne peeled some notes out of her bag.

"U.S. dollars." The youth's eyes lit up as he reached for them.

The taxi driver started to protest, Jayne handed him the next set of notes. "You can leave me here." She'd had enough of his driving.

"But the palace?" He looked suddenly nervous.

Jayne waved a hand. "Don't worry about taking me to the palace." She'd have a better chance of surviving on her own. Jayne looked left and right, hitched her handbag over her shoulder and grabbed the handle of her suitcase.

Down the street she could see the flower *souq*, the market where blooms were brought early each morning. Across the road a pension-style hotel attracted her eye. It looked modest and unassuming, the kind of place where a woman alone would be safe from unwelcome attention. She could stay there for the night. And tomorrow she'd be better prepared to face Tariq, rested and refreshed. She started to feel better.

A hand brushed her arm. Jayne tensed and spun around,

then relaxed. The taxi driver thrust a grimy square of cardboard at her. Jayne glanced down. Mohammed al Dubarik and a scrawl of Arabic characters followed by some numbers that clearly belonged to his cell phone. With a final flash of yellowed teeth and bright gold, he departed in a roar of dust.

Jayne shoved the card into her bag and looked both ways then hefted up her bag to cross the street. The curious crowd, sensing the drama was played out, started to disperse. Pulling the chiffon scarf more securely over her head she made for the door of the pension. She'd almost reached it when a touch on her shoulder startled her.

At first she thought the taxi driver had returned.

She turned her head…and saw the youth who had fallen off the bicycle. Standing, he looked a whole lot bigger. And far more threatening with the gang of faces that loomed behind him. With no chickens and no bike, he suddenly didn't look so young and vulnerable. In fact, he looked downright menacing.

And then she saw the knife.

Jayne screamed. The sound was cut off midutterance as the biggest youth moved with the speed of a striking snake and shoved her up against the rough plaster wall of the pension. Through the tinted glass door, Jayne glimpsed an elderly man inside the pension, behind the reception desk, he caught her eye and looked away.

No help from that quarter.

Fear set in like a bird fluttering frantically within her chest. "Please, don't hurt—"

A screech of brakes. A shout of a familiar voice in Arabic. Then she was free.

Jayne heard the sound of feet rushing along the sun-baked sidewalk, caught a glimpse of khaki and red uniforms giving chase.

"Jayne!"

She knew that voice. Recalled it from her most shattering dreams…and her worst nightmares. She sagged against the rough plastered wall of the pension as Tariq leapt from the Mercedes, shutting her eyes, blocking him out. *All of him.* The lithe body that moved with the fluidity of a big cat, the hawk-like features that had hardened with the passage of the years, the golden eyes that were molten with a terrible anger.

"Get in."

"I want—"

"I don't care what you want." The molten eyes turned to flame. *"Get into the car."*

To her astonishment, Jayne found herself obeying. The Mercedes smelled of leather, of wealth and a hint of the spicy aftershave that Tariq wore—had always worn. The scent wove memories of Tariq close to her, holding her, of his skin under her lips. She shrank into the corner and curled away from the unwelcome memories. Memories that she had come here to excise forever. By getting a divorce.

"Look at me."

She turned her head. His face was set in stone. Hard. Bleak as the desert. Until she detected a tangle of swirling emotions in his eyes. Not all of which she could identify. There was anger. Frustration. And other emotions, too. Dark emotions that she'd hoped never to see again.

Two

"So, you decided to avoid the welcome I had planned for you." As the Mercedes pulled away, Tariq delivered the statement in a flat, emotionless tone, despite the rage that seethed inside him at what had nearly happened to her.

"Welcome?" Jayne laughed. It was not a happy sound. Annoyingly, she looked away from him again and he couldn't read her eyes—the eyes that had always given away her every emotion. "You would be the last person I'd expect to welcome me anywhere."

"I am your husband. It is my duty to welcome you to Zayed."

Jayne didn't respond.

"Why did you run?" He didn't like the fact that she had taken one look at him in the airport and fled. Whatever else lay between them in the past, Jayne had never feared him. Nor was he happy with the notion that the only reason she was in the car was because he was the lesser of two evils. The thought that she considered his company only a notch above that of the youths who had assaulted her turned his mouth sour.

"I wasn't dressed for the occasion."

Anger rose at her flippant response and he pressed his lips into a thin line. Was she so unmoved by the attack? He knew that it would prey on his mind for a long time to come. He had thought that he had no feeling left for his errant wife, that her actions had killed every feeling he'd ever nurtured for her. But the instant he had seen that young dog lay his hand on Jayne, rage—and something else—had rushed through him. He could rationalise the anger, the blind red mist of rage.

She was his woman.

No other man had any right to touch her. Ever.

What he couldn't understand was his concern for Jayne, the woman who had behaved so atrociously in the past. He couldn't understand this urge to make such woman feel safe, to assure her that what had happened out there in the back-streets of Jazirah wasn't her fault. Even though it would never have happened if she had graciously accepted the welcome he'd arranged.

Before he could work through the confusing threads, Jayne was speaking again, "I don't intend to stay long. A big welcome like the one you arranged would give the wrong impression and suggest that I've returned to stay." She shrugged. "I thought it for the best to leave."

"The best for whom? You? It certainly did me no good to be left standing there looking like a fool."

"You would never look like a fool. But I would've. I was

ill prepared for the occasion. How do you think I would've looked…sounded…on national television?"

Tariq swept his gaze over her, taking in the tension in every line of her body, the way the cheap clothes stuck to her in the heat, the dishevelled hair revealed under the scanty *hijab* that had fallen away and the white-knuckled hands clasped on her lap. Perhaps she wasn't as composed as she sounded. Perhaps the attack had shaken her. In the old days she would've come apart, started to cry, she'd been so gentle, with her huge, adoring, doelike brown eyes. It had been her gentleness that had caused him to love her. There had been so little tenderness in his own life.

"What are you looking at? I'm sorry if I'm not wearing haute couture. I'm sorry if you think I'm unfit for your company."

There was an unfamiliar note of annoyance in her voice, and resentment flashed in her eyes. Tariq blinked in astonishment. Where had this come from? Jayne had always been easygoing and eager to please, hero-worshipping him. "Unfit for my company?" he repeated. "I have never thought that. I married you, didn't I?"

She ran a hand over her face. "Look, I feel like I've been flying forever. I'm tired, cranky. The last thing I wanted was a welcome reception with TV cameras, for heaven's sake."

"Your apology is accepted."

He waited and watched the wide brown eyes flash again. He almost smiled. Yes, he could get used to this.

"It wasn't an apology, it was an explanation why I am less civil than normal." Her voice was curt. "You should not have sprung that surprise on me. And as for what's best for me, yes, in the past our relationship was always about what you and your fa—family wanted. I didn't need that circus back there at the airport. I came here for one reason only, to talk. With you. Alone. To get a divorce. I didn't want to be welcomed back as your sheikhah. That would be a lie, because I have no intention of staying."

Tariq gave her a long, level glance. She wanted a divorce. Three months ago he'd have been too eager to grant her that, he would have been grateful to have the gentle, malleable wife, who he tried so hard never to think about, out of his life. But then everything had changed. His father was far from well. He needed her in Zayed at his side. And after his response to her attack and seeing the new flash of fire in her, he was not sure that he'd be letting her go too quickly.

For the first time in his life he was confused. And he didn't like that bewildering sensation at all.

The palace lay ahead of them, dazzling, stupendous. The sandstone had been bleached over the centuries to a warm and inviting shade of gold. A mirage. Because Jayne knew that behind the walls lay a world of intrigue, politics…and the cold heart of the Emir who had destroyed her.

They drove around the side and under the rising wrought-iron portcullis into a large courtyard paved with cobbles where the Mercedes slowed to a stop. The driver opened her door and Jayne alighted.

Even now, with her confidence rebuilt after more than five long years away, she felt apprehensive as she entered the immense vaulted hallway through the side door.

"I'd like to call my sister to let her know I arrived safely." Jayne craved the reassurance of Helen's no-nonsense voice.

"Of course."

She thought of Samantha's request for photos. "And is there somewhere I can use for e-mail?"

"Yes, my study is available to you at any time."

"Thank you." She directed a small smile up at him.

Tariq went still. His eyes glinted as he came closer. "Jayne—"

"Excellency, it is good that you are back." The interruption came from an aide wearing a worried frown. "Sheikh Tariq, there is need for your presence. Sheikh Ali has arrived demanding an audience. He has brought Sheikh Mahood, and they have been waiting for you." The aide was wringing his hands.

Tariq moved away. Jayne felt his withdrawal, and it left a chill, cold feeling in her chest. Her heart sank further at the mention of Sheikh Ali. That was another name she would never have regretted not hearing in her lifetime again. She sneaked a sideways glance at Tariq.

His face had darkened. "Tell them that I will be with them shortly."

"I've already told them that you were welcoming the sheikhah back after a long absence. They do not care about that, they are only concerned about the issue of grazing rights in the northern territories."

Jayne flinched at Tariq's short, sharp curse. Then he turned to her. "I need to go. I will see you at dinner." Tariq's voice was brisk, businesslike. "We will talk further then. In the meantime, Latifa will show you to your apartments."

Jayne hadn't heard the woman's silent approach. Her face was round with the plumpness of youth, her eyes wide and respectful as she gazed at Jayne, waiting for instruction.

"Wait—" Jayne called after Tariq, but he didn't hear, because his pace picked up as he strode away to attend to the latest crisis in Zayed, his head bent to listen to the aide beside him.

A sense of loss ebbed through Jayne. She forced it back with effort and turned to the young woman who waited respectfully. "Thank you, Latifa. I'd appreciate it if you showed me to my room. I'm looking forward to freshening up."

It turned out to be a vast boudoir with stone arched windows that looked out onto the lush palace gardens filled with date palms, fountains and the clinging fragrance of honeysuckle and gardenia.

Jayne kicked off her shoes and toured around the rooms, exploring the crannies before making her way to the large bathroom where Latifa had filled the enormous spa bath. The sweet scent of the crushed rose petals was inviting…intoxicating. One of those little luxuries that seeped the ache out of the soul, made the daily misery of life in Zayed seem bearable.

Ten minutes later, lying back in the sleek, scented water, the realisation that she was back here in Tariq's world, where she'd sworn never to return, sank in.

Jayne wondered whether there would be chance to talk with Tariq later. Her husband was an important man. He was no figurehead sheikh. His father had always demanded his full involvement in the affairs of the state that he would one day head. Not that the Emir would be in any hurry to relinquish control of his rule.

In the past the demands on Tariq's time had driven a wedge between them. And Jayne was relieved that on this visit it was not her problem. She no longer needed Tariq to fulfil the role of husband and lover. All she required was sufficient time to discuss his enigmatic statement:

"There will be no divorce. Not yet. But it is possible that the time will come soon. Very soon. We will talk."

She wasn't accepting that kiss-off. She had come to Zayed for a divorce. The time was here. She would not allow Tariq to dominate her as he had done in the past. She'd grown up; she was no longer in awe of her powerful husband.

A long soak left her body feeling heavy and languid. At last Jayne summoned the energy to get out of the bath and, wrapped in a soft ivory towel, she made her way back to the sumptuous bedroom where her meagre selection of clothing had been packed into the cupboard by Latifa.

Mindful of the conservative nature of the palace, Jayne chose a long black skirt that clung to her hips before falling to just above her ankles and teamed it with a black top with a vee-neck and long, trumpet-shaped sheer chiffon sleeves. A pair of ballet-style black pumps and she was as ready as she'd ever be to face Tariq.

Downstairs she was surprised to find only Tariq waiting for her in the small salon. He'd shed the dark designer suit and wore a traditional white *thobe*. It added to his height, emphasised his dark, hawklike features and made him appear more imposing than ever. Jayne hesitated in the doorway. "Where is everyone?"

In the past, facing a room full of strangers she barely knew at the end of the day over the long dinner table had been one of the major strains of life in the palace. Aides and distant family members of the Emir, members of desert clans, all came to the palace to seek advice from the Emir or one of the senior members of the ruling family. And she'd expected the delegation Tariq had met with about the grazing rights earlier today to be here.

"My father is…not well. Many are keeping vigil in the courtyard and antechamber outside his rooms."

"Oh." For a brief moment Jayne considered asking what was wrong with the Emir, then she decided against it. It would be too direct a question. Too impolite. And then there was the fact that she was reluctant to become embroiled in an argument with Tariq about his father. Which was where any innocent, well-meaning query would end. Instead she focused on what she'd come for. "Can we talk about finalising the divorce?"

"After dinner," Tariq said. "You have been travelling, you will need sustenance."

"I'll be fine, this won't take long." She glanced at him with a frown. He was prevaricating. That was a palace etiquette rule, if it would raise conflict, a matter could not be aired during a meal. "I can't believe you forced me to fly across the world to talk about a divorce to which I am entitled."

His expression became distant. "You are not entitled to it, not until I give my consent."

She gave a snort of disgust. "Surely you're not going to take that line. It's antiquated. If this is about your male pride, then *you* may divorce *me*. I don't care. You needn't have dragged me across the world for this."

His eyes were hooded. "You will be recompensed for any…inconvenience."

"That's not necessary." She raised her chin. She didn't need his money. "All I want is the divorce. That will be worth every cent of the trip."

His brows jerked together. "You will get your divorce. When I am ready. But now we eat."

Jayne found herself bristling at the command. But she forced herself to take a deep breath and follow him through the French doors onto the terrace outside. Stairs cut into a wall of stone, lined with flaming sconces, led to a secret garden where white flowers bloomed in the waning light. In the arbour, surrounded with white roses, a table had been laid and an array of food spread out.

Nearby a fountain tinkled, the sound of water calming Jayne's frazzled nerves.

There was huge platter of fruit with dates and wedges of crumbly white cheese that resembled *haloumi.* Another plate held a selection of flatbreads with hummus, fried *kibbe,* the spicy meatballs with pine nuts, and a dish of tabbouleh salad. Eyeing the spread, Jayne discovered that she was hungrier than she'd thought.

"Is that falafel?" she pointed to a plate of patties.

"*Ta'amiyya.* It's made with fava beans, but it's not dissimilar to falafel. Try some."

Jayne did. She selected a little of everything and let Tariq pour her a glass of icy water. After she'd finished eating, Tariq selected two peaches from the fruit bowl to the side of the table. Picking up a sharp knife he deftly cut the peaches into slices. The inner flesh was a ripe golden orange and the juice dripped from his fingertips.

He offered her the plate.

"Oh, I couldn't, I pigged out."

"Try them. The taste is sweet, the flesh of the fruit soft and succulent. They were flown in from Damascus today."

He made them sound utterly irresistible. Against her better judgment, Jayne reached out and took a sliver. Tasted it. The peach lived up to everything he had promised.

"Like it?"

"Mmm."

His eyes grew darker at her throaty murmur. "You used to make delighted sounds like that when we made love."

"I don't remember."

"Of course you do." Tariq's eyes were hooded, but his voice was softer than velvet and caused little shivers to spread through her.

The meal was over. She no longer had to observe social niceties. It was time for a little directness. "I don't *want* to remember. I want to go back home, to move on with my life."

"There was a time when your home was with me—"

She waved a hand, dismissing his claim. "That was another life."

"So, there is another man…at this new home?"

"I didn't say that." But Jayne couldn't help thinking of Neil, who had waited so patiently, asking her out every couple of weeks, taking her refusals stoically. He was so safe. So different from her overwhelming husband—and that was precisely what made Neil so attractive. He wouldn't take her to the highs or the lows that Tariq had. He wouldn't crush her love and her trust and rip her heart out.

"I have no doubt that the sudden urge for the divorce is linked to a man." Tariq's savage cynicism took her aback.

"Why does it have to be about a man? I want to move on, get a life." Jayne swallowed under his quelling gaze. "I want my identity as Jayne Jones back. I no longer want to be associated with you, Sheikh Tariq bin Rashid al Zayed, son of the Emir of Zayed."

The look he shot her was deadly. "I hadn't realised I was such a liability."

"Surely you want to move on, too? Get married? Have children?"

"Maybe." His face gave nothing away.

A sharp stab of emotion pierced her. His father had wanted Tariq to marry Leila, the daughter of one of the sheikhs who had arrived at the palace earlier today. Both men were counted amongst the Emir's closest friends. Sheikh Ali was a power in the north of the country. He owned extensive land, controlled oil leases and governed several, at times, unruly clans. And Leila's uncle, Sheikh Mahood, was related by marriage to a sultan who ruled a bordering state that put out a massive amount of barrels of oil per day. Tariq's marriage to Leila would solidify the fate of Zayed, making the tiny country more powerful and strategic in the region.

No doubt that marriage would take place once their divorce was final.

"On the way from the airport you said that in the past our relationship was always about what I wanted, about what my family wanted. That it wasn't about you. I don't remember it that way." His voice lowered to throb a little above a murmur. "In fact, I remember sitting on a hard park bench in London, not far from that awful one-bedroom flat we rented, and staring into your eyes while we talked about the future and shared our dreams. It was about us. Not me. Not my family."

How dare he remind her of those long-ago days? She'd been so young, so in love with the gorgeous student she'd met at the Tate Gallery. Too soon they'd been married. A mad, later regretted, impulse. "Our marriage was a mistake."

Before his world and the reality of who he was—the Emir of Zayed's only son—had come crashing in on them. Memories of the bittersweet days when he'd loved her—and she'd loved him—with youthful joyfulness haunted her. Then the long shadow of his father, the Emir of Zayed, had raised its head. Tariq had been summoned back to his father's control and overnight everything had changed.

He had changed.

Jayne's fingernails bit into her palms. She'd changed, back then, too. She'd gone from sensitive to wan and needy. And that had been before the discovery that—

"We were happy," he interrupted her thoughts. "For a while."

"Until I found out who you were, and everything changed." She took a long, hard look at him. He was still the most earth-shatteringly gorgeous male she'd ever met. His golden eyes glowed with intelligence. His high, slanting cheekbones, the arrogant blade of his nose above the chiselled lips, still had the power to make her heart race. But, clad in the *thobe*, the fearsomely muscled body hidden beneath the white folds, he looked foreign, dangerous and very, very powerful.

"Who I was should never have changed what we had."

"Oh, come on, Tariq. You can't honestly believe that? The pressure of being the successor to the Emir of Zayed, the hostility of your father—"

"Leave my father out of this!" His face darkened. "He never did anything to harm you. It was your behaviour, your treachery, that destroyed what we had."

Jayne shut her eyes blocking out the familiar invective. The Emir had hated her from the start, done everything he could to break up what they shared. And, in the end he'd succeeded. She'd been driven away, her spirit beaten, her heart broken.

Tariq had hated her.

"What does the past matter? You say it was my treachery that drove us apart. But in the end it was your lack of trust that killed what we had, Tariq. So what's the point of—"

"My lack of trust?" Fury turned the body beside her to steel. "You—"

"There's no point to all this, Tariq." She turned her head and stared at the water bubbling from the fountainhead. "It's over. I want a divorce…and once I leave I never want to see you or your father again."

"You may just get your wish." He drew a deep breath. "My father is dying."

Jayne heard his words from a distance; they didn't sound quite real. Six years ago she'd wished that the old Emir could…simply disappear out of her life…out of Tariq's life. Then, his death would have solved all her problems. Yet now she didn't care.

She felt numb. She told herself it was because she'd moved on. She had a life. And that life did not include Tariq. Not even if his father was dying.

"What does that have to do with me?" She kept her voice expressionless. "I don't care about your father. I don't care if he's dying." She swallowed her pain and flicked him a look. A flash of raw emotion glittered in his eyes. It was quickly suppressed. Her throat closed, feeling hot and tight. "I have no desire to see your father. Not ever again. When you told me to leave five and a half years ago, I told you that."

"You said you never wanted to see me, either." His mouth kinked into a mocking line. "Yet here you sit, in front of me. So, *nuur il-en,* never is a long time. Death has a finality that comes to us all. My father feels it is time for me to settle— he wants that reassurance before he dies."

He paused. The silence swelled darkly around them, coloured by the undercurrents between them.

"So?"

"Who better for me to settle with than my lawfully wedded wife?"

Jayne gave an uncontrollable laugh. It was hard and grating. Alien. As alien as the notion that the Emir would ever accept her as the consort for his son. "That's the last thing your father wants. He'd prefer to see me in hell." She gave him a twisted smile. "What about Leila? Why not settle down with her? Your father would approve that match like a shot."

"Unfortunately, Leila is now married. I do not approve of bigamy."

Unexpectedly, Jayne's heart lifted at the information. Then she quashed her exultation. It had nothing to do with her, who he married. "So divorce me and find another bride."

"There is no time. My father needs to be assured that I am married, happily reconciled with you. Now. And you are going to help me achieve that. As soon as he is dead you can leave. With this divorce you want so badly."

There was something savagely ironic at the idea that Tariq wanted her aid to deceive his father into thinking he was settled. But she had no intention of staying. She shook her head. "I want you to sign the consent to our divorce, then I want to leave."

"You never used to be this hard of heart—"

"Me? Hard-hearted?"

"You used to be gentle, loving." Tariq continued.

"Until you and your father got hold of me."

Tariq's gaze turned dark with bitterness. "Don't blame—"

"Oh, what is the use?" She wasn't going to get through to him. She gave a dismissive shrug. "I don't care anymore what you think of me. I've grown up. I don't need your approval anymore."

Tariq's lips thinned into a hard line. "But you do want a

divorce. And I'm not signing anything unless you stay. So unless you convince my father all is well between us before he dies, I will not consent to a divorce. Ever."

"I'll sue for divorce from New Zealand."

"And I'll oppose you. Even though our marriage was recorded at the New Zealand High Commission in London at the time, we were married according to the laws of Zayed and I am a citizen of that country. You need my consent. I have a lot of money to fight you with. And you know that I will succeed. Otherwise you would have applied for divorce in New Zealand. Not come all the way here to persuade me to give you this divorce."

He had her there. "Tariq, what you're asking is impossible."

Tariq glanced at his wife and suppressed the tenderness that threatened to spill out. She looked bewildered, off balance for the first time since her arrival. Not even when she'd been faced by those young thugs had she looked as shattered. She'd remained calm, unflustered, sitting beside him with her long lashes lowered against the porcelain skin he'd always relished, while he'd simmered with rage that any one dared touch his woman.

He'd wanted to arrest the youth, have him expelled from Zayed for touching Jayne. He'd fought the red, red rage for calm.

And in that instant he'd known that he was going to make this divorce as difficult as he could. But none of the seething emotion was revealed when he said, "I am not asking the impossible. It is my wish, dearest beloved—"

"Don't call me that. I am no longer your dearest beloved."

"That is true. You are no longer *my* dearest beloved." He knew she'd recognised his point by the way her body tensed against his. But he was not yet ready to open the wounds of the past. "Stay until my father dies. That is the last thing I ask of you, my wife—" he paused, waiting for her to respond to the subtle mockery, but her lashes again swept her cheeks "—before I grant you the divorce you seek so urgently."

He watched as she examined her nails. They were short, bare of polish. "How long?"

At her question his head came up. He narrowed his gaze, searching her averted face for guile. "What do you mean, 'How long'?"

"How long…must I stay?"

"Until my father dies."

"Yes…I know…but how long will that be?"

Something constricted in his chest as she flouted the conventions that frowned on such directness. Tariq felt a burning sense of…frustration…that she so clearly wanted out of their marriage, that she was prepared to ask him to quantify how many days remained for his father in this realm. He shrugged. "How long is a piece of thread?"

"That's no answer." At last she looked at him. "I want a time limit."

"I don't know." He stared at her, brooding. Hoped she didn't see all the way to his soul to the dark, black well of sorrow and confusion that lay there. "The thread of his life is close to snapping. He is very weak and in much pain. The doctors say it could be a week or two weeks. They don't give him longer than a month."

"A month!" She hesitated, her eyelashes lowered again. Her teeth closed on her bottom lip.

He waited, giving her time. She was impatient. Tariq narrowed his gaze on her teeth, the endearing gap between them, and wondered what it was about this Neil that had her so enthralled that she'd come back to the country she'd sworn never to return to, to get her divorce. The pictures of the man, procured from the detective agency he'd hired immediately after her call to his father's aide, showed an ordinary-looking man with a thatch of blond hair and an innocuous smile. Nothing pointed to Jayne having a sexual relationship with this man, this Neil.

Yet.

Right now that was the only thing keeping Tariq sane.

He had banished her. But he had not yet divorced her. He, Sheikh Tariq bin Rashid al Zayed, *owned* her. And what he owned he kept. Until he decided to rid himself of the troubling possession. As he would.

After his father died.

At last she looked up at him, her eyes darkened by shadows of turmoil. Her features pinched and drawn, a woman driven beyond her limits.

"Okay, I'll stay. But not for more than a month. I want your word on that. If your father hasn't…" Her voice trailed away.

"Died?" he supplied.

"Yes." She paused and shifted, looking dreadfully uncomfortable with the direction the conversation had taken. Then it came out with a rush. "Even if he hasn't…well…died, I want to go home in a month. I want you to swear you will give me a divorce."

It was time to cut her a little slack. It was extremely doubtful that his father would survive that long. "You have my word. Stay for the month and you will get the divorce you desire." Tariq allowed his voice to soften. "You will find my father…changed. He's very ill. He has moments when the medication takes effect and he is not himself." It pained Tariq that his strong father was so frail, so weak, in his body and his mind. It devastated him that disease had crept up undetected on the seemingly invulnerable Emir. "For that month you must promise me that you will strive to convince my father in his lucid moments that we are reconciled."

She drew a deep breath, then whispered, "I promise."

Three

The following morning Jayne crept silently into the Emir's quarters. A couple of men huddled in the antechamber murmuring prayers and didn't notice her sneaking past. The male nurse in the bedchamber nodded to Jayne as she entered.

Jayne was shocked at the change in the tyrant who had made her life such a misery. Sheikh Rashid lay in the high bed, his face gaunt, the bones showing through skin as pale as parchment, his lips drained of all colour. He turned his head when she paused beside him. Jayne had a glimpse of rheumy eyes, great black sunken rings around them, and then his eyelids closed again.

"He is not well today," the nurse said. "He has been drifting in and out of consciousness, confused about what is real and what is not. The painkillers are not helping."

"What exactly is wrong with him?" Jayne asked delicately.

"He has cancer of the bowel. It has been eating him, sapping his vitality."

So it was true. The old Emir really was dying. But Jayne felt no satisfaction…or even regret. Instead, a searing sadness followed by a vast well of emptiness filled her.

"I'm so sorry."

Sheikh Rashid's eyes opened. For a moment there was a flare of recognition. Jayne recoiled. The Emir muttered something indistinct.

"He is talking to you," the nurse said. "Bend closer."

Wary, as if he could bite, Jayne moved closer. She leaned forward.

"Lina," she thought he whispered.

Jayne frowned. "He's saying something." She waited a moment, then reached out awkwardly and touched the pile of bedclothes. "I am here."

"Lina," he whispered more insistently.

Her eyes troubled, Jayne said to the nurse, "I think he is confusing me with someone else." She patted the bedclothes, feeling the bony shoulder through the coverings.

His eyelids fluttered down and his breathing became regular.

"He's sleeping. Your presence is soothing him."

There must be some mistake. If he knew about her presence, the Emir would be rabid with rage. Withdrawing her hand, Jayne backed away to the door.

When Jayne went searching for Tariq a little while later, the disturbing sense of unease aroused by her visit to the Emir still had not left her. She found Tariq in the mews where the royal raptors were housed. Squinting through the dim light to the back of the building, Jayne made out Tariq's form clad in his distinctive white *thobe*.

She picked her way past a row of hooded birds perched on railings. There had been times in the past when she'd thought the birds were accorded more respect and affection than she had been.

The falcon perched regally on Tariq's glove glowered at her with suspicious eyes that reminded her instantly of Tariq—even though these were dark and his were pure gold. It was a larger bird than she'd expected to see. But the bird had the same long, pointed wings and dark eyes.

"That's not Khan," Jayne said, referring to Tariq's prized bird. The bird gaped at her, its beak open, a show of aggression to an unfamiliar intruder.

"This is Noor, a young bird that I'm training. Like Khan, she's a shaheen—a peregrine—but she doesn't know you."

"She's bigger." Jayne eyed the bird's open mouth with caution. The feathers on the falcon's head and neck were black, and a dark stripe extended down from the eye to the throat. Noor's throat and cheeks were white with narrow banded stripes on her breast and flecks across her back.

"She's a female, they're up to a third larger than the males. Here." Tariq passed Jayne a small piece of meat. "Place it in her open beak. It will stop her threatening you."

Jayne fed the bird gingerly, wary of the sharp beak. When the titbit was gone, Noor tilted her head expectantly. "No more for now," Jayne told the bird. To Tariq she said, "Where's Khan?"

"Khan died. A long time ago." The shadows in his eyes told her he was thinking of more than his beloved falcon.

Jayne could prevaricate no longer. "Your father is much worse than I expected."

"I told you that he is dying."

"I didn't—" She broke off. *I didn't believe you.* "I didn't realise how bad it was. The nurse said that he has cancer."

Tariq nodded. "He fought it with everything he had. He has lost the most important battle of his life."

"I'm sorry."

The words sounded so inadequate.

Tariq must have thought so, too, because he raised a mocking brow. "I doubt it. You always hated him."

Jayne stared at him mutely. Now was hardly the time to correct him, to tell him that Sheikh Rashid had hated *her* with a ferocious intensity that had sometimes scared her witless. The Emir had seen her as an interloper, and had taken every opportunity to make her feel like an outsider, until he'd poisoned even Tariq against her.

The falcon shifted restlessly on the glove, bringing Jayne's attention back to the bird. She studied the leather jesses bound to her legs. Noor was as captive as she had once been. "Noor wants your attention."

"She's hungry. She wants food." Tariq moved his other hand into the bucket containing strips of meat. The falcon tensed, her head coming forward, anticipation in every line of her body. Tariq placed the piece of meat on the glove and the falcon lowered her head and took it.

"Here, give her another piece."

Jayne fed it to the bird. This time Noor gave a squawk. Jayne gave the bird a wary look.

"She won't eat you." There was a hint of derision in his tone. "It's easy to come to an understanding with a falcon. The falcon simply has to stay hungrier."

Noor gaped at her again. "I don't think she likes me."

Tariq made an impatient sound. "She's a bird. Noor doesn't recognise like or love. She's interested in having her wants satisfied. She feels no emotion." He shot her a hooded glance. "A typical woman."

Jayne ignored the dig. "She's so graceful yet so strong." She moved to stroke the bird, Noor flapped her wings in warning.

"Careful. She's a wild animal, a predator. An opportunist. Not a house pet."

"Is she hungry? Will you take her out to hunt? Or will she fly away?"

"She's eaten sufficient. But even if I took her out she would not fly away. My relationship with Noor is straightforward, based on trust—unlike most male-female interactions. Noor trusts me to feed her. I trust her to return."

Jayne felt the jab of the barb. She started to protest. Then gave up. She wasn't going to allow herself to be drawn. Instead she said, "Your father spoke to me."

Tariq's gaze sharpened. "What did he say?"

"I couldn't make out what he was saying. I think he was confused, he thought I was someone else. He called me 'Lina.'"

His head went back, and his eyes flared to black. "That's impossible. You must've misheard."

Jayne considered him. What was that stark emotion in his eyes? Shock? Disbelief. And why? "What does it mean?"

"That was his name for my mother." Tariq's eyes were as empty as the stony desert she'd passed in the taxi yesterday.

"Perhaps he wants to see her?"

"No." He made a sudden, definite movement. The falcon reacted by flapping her wings and hopping up and down on the glove. "My mother is not welcome in Zayed."

Jayne waited. When Tariq failed to add more, she said, "I never met your mother. You never talk about her."

"As far as my father and I are concerned, that woman does not exist."

"Yet you see your maternal cousins, don't you?"

"That is different. Not only are we bound by blood, we are bound by business interests, too. My cousin Zac owns supertankers, I run refineries. There's a reason for us to get together. My cousins know that my mother is not welcome in my presence."

"Well, I don't think that's how your father feels any longer. He's dying. Perhaps he wants to make peace with your mother."

"My mother abandoned us—him—for another man. She has her own family—another daughter."

There was a flatness to Tariq's tone that had Jayne shooting him a questioning look. There must be pain about his mother's desertion. Somewhere. Deep inside him. They'd been married, yet she'd never been aware of this suffering within him.

"There is no space in her life for me or my father," he said, feeding Noor another sliver of meat. "Nor would my father want her back."

"Perhaps it's not a case of wanting her back. Perhaps it's more about wanting to tie off the loose ends in his life before he dies."

"You misheard. My father would never want my mother back in Zayed." The finality in Tariq's tone warned Jayne that the subject of his mother was better left alone.

Absently Jayne watched the bird preen, her beak stroking through her feathers, setting them right. "I'm sorry I mentioned it. I just thought you might know who your father confused me with."

"It doesn't surprise me that he confused you." A hand touched her hair. Jayne's gaze jerked upward. Emotion flared in his eyes. "You both have long, dark hair and pale ivory skin."

"I've never seen a photo of your mother." Jayne was sure his mother would be beautiful. Nothing like her. Ordinary. Plain Jayne.

"There are no pictures in the palace of my mother. As there are none of you. Both of you treacherous, two-timing—"

Jayne shifted abruptly. "I'm not listening to this. I was prepared to discuss this in the past. You wouldn't listen then and I'm not getting caught up in it all over again." He'd stonewalled her then, breaking her heart. "It's water under the bridge."

Water under the bridge.

The painful memories exploded inside her. She swung away from Tariq and made blindly for the exit to the mews, to where shafts of silver sunlight broke into the gloomy interior, lighting her escape. No footsteps followed. And she was glad.

She didn't want to talk about the baby that she'd carried in her body. The baby she'd lost. It hurt too much. It was something she could never forget, something that stayed with her every day of her life.

But what choice had she had?

The day dragged past. Jayne had bought some magazines at the airport in Auckland to read on the plane and she flicked through them listlessly. She itched for a book to read, but Tariq's library was a place she dared not go. It held too many unpleasant reminders of his distrust.

So she lay down on the bed and dozed, until every last wisp of jetlag had lifted. When the knock sounded on the door late in the afternoon, heralding Latifa's entrance, Jayne was ready for a distraction.

"There are many people in the palace this evening. His Excellency has been kept busy all day." Latifa's young eyes were kind and wise beyond their years. "I am sure Sheikh Tariq is looking forward to seeing the sheikhah tonight. There has been much talking today."

This was what had driven her mad the first time round. The long days with no sign of Tariq. The absence of anything to do, while the men closed themselves behind high carved wooden doors, wearing sombre expressions. And few of the women she'd met had spoken English, even though some had seemed nice enough. But apart from one or two invitations none had made any overtures of friendship to her.

In the past Tariq had told her to be patient. That she would make friends in time, that her loneliness would ease.

If only it had been so simple.

"Look, this came for you today." Latifa produced the box with the air of a magician performing a wondrous trick that deserved squeals of delight. Jayne didn't have the heart not to smile.

"What is it?"

"It is most beautiful." Latifa opened the lid to reveal a caftan and sheer *hijab* in shades of emerald shot through with bronze thread. "There are shoes to match and pants." She pulled out the high-heeled pumps like a rabbit from a hat. "And more clothes will arrive in the morning."

"I don't want clothes," Jayne protested.

But once dressed, Jayne had to admit that the colour suited her. The green accentuated the raven highlights in her hair, and her skin was paler than ever. Mascara, and a hint of *kajal* around her eyes to emphasise the shape, and she was ready to go. Draping the *hijab* across her shoulders and leaving her hair uncovered, she made her way downstairs, through the labyrinth of palace corridors.

The long table in the stateroom was laid with cutlery that gleamed in the light of the heavy chandeliers overhead. Men from the large delegation that Latifa had alluded to were already arriving; some in dark suits with only the traditional headgear, while others wore traditional dress. A few women were scattered around. A quick glance revealed that Tariq was nowhere to be seen.

An aide appeared and directed Jayne to where two vacant seats remained down the length of the table. Jayne kept her head down, aware of the speculative glances she was attracting. She was grateful for the welcoming smile from the woman seated to the left of her and they started to chat.

The woman introduced herself as Farrah Jirah in fluent English. It turned out that she was a doctor who practised in the maternity unit of the local hospital. Jayne found her charming, and she stopped worrying about where Tariq was.

When Tariq finally strode in, flanked by Ali and Mahood, Jayne could tell from the taut way he held himself that the latest round of meetings had not gone well.

Tariq's gaze flashed to the top of the table, took in the empty place at the head. His brow drew into a frown as he scanned the surrounding seats. The tension in his shoulders relaxed slightly when he saw her.

Jayne turned back to talk to her friendly neighbour. A moment later she sensed someone beside her.

"Are you okay?"

It was Tariq. He looked tired, the lines around his mouth

more deeply scored than they had been this morning, and his eyes held concern.

"I'm fine. You look tired."

A ghost of a smile flitted over his harsh features. "It's been a hard day."

"I won't even ask how whatever meetings you had went." Ali and Mahood were trouble. Vipers. She'd known that since the first time she'd met them. And Ali's daughter, Leila, was pure poison. Tariq was welcome to her.

Tariq sighed and said softly, "Ali is a powerful force in Zayed."

Jayne nodded. Ali controlled a lot of the northern territory, making him an important player.

"He can't be ignored," Tariq continued. "But he is disruptive. And this latest skirmish Ali and Mahood have gotten into over grazing rights with Sheikh Karim al Bashir is going to cause headaches."

"Are they fighting?"

"It hasn't turned violent yet. But Ali claims that Sheikh Karim is threatening war." Impatience showed in Tariq's eyes. "The sooner I intervene, the better."

Jayne felt a flutter of pity for him, for the predicament that Ali and his brother had put Tariq in. "But what about your father? You can't leave him now."

"My father wouldn't want this disagreement to flare out of control. We can't afford to be at war with Bashir. He will understand."

"Why can't Ali and Mahood understand that you're needed here?"

He looked at her. "No one understands that. Only you. To every one else my duty to Zayed must come before all else—

even my father. And now you must excuse me, *nuur il-en,* I must claim my seat at the head of the table before Ali usurps it."

Ali was sitting in the vacant chair at the top of the table, his head close to the man on his right, conspiring no doubt. Jayne shifted her attention to Tariq, watched him rise from beside her, his traditional robes swirling around him, the white *ghutra* over his head secured by the doubled black cord that made him look more formidable than ever. She pitied Ali and Mahood if they unleashed his full ire.

She picked at her food until she sensed someone seating themselves in the place Tariq had vacated, and turned her head. The welcoming smile she'd prepared shrivelled as she met the frigid gaze of Sheikh Ali.

The dinner dragged on and Tariq found it difficult to concentrate on the conversation swirling around him. His attention was riveted on his wife. He watched as she said something to Ali. But the response caused her to sag. What had Ali said to make her skin grow so pale?

As the meal progressed his attention kept straying back. Most of the time Jayne spent chatting to the woman on her left, Dr. Farrah Jirah was a nice enough woman and he'd hoped she might befriend Jayne. He relaxed as he saw Jayne smile. But then stiffened again when he noted that the few times she attempted to talk to Ali her attempts were rebuffed. Ali was flouting the social norms of Zayedi politeness at a meal table. As host, Tariq was within his rights to request Ali to leave. Tariq's frown grew more and more thunderous, until his dinner partners started to regard him with increasing wariness.

Ali said something to Jayne. She glanced down, and Tariq

saw the wash of colour high on her ivory cheeks. He started to rise. But Jayne beat him to it. Pushing back her chair, she was on her feet before he could move. By the time he reached the elaborate carved doors flanked by two palace guards, she was already gone.

He charged into the corridor, saw her disappearing into the study he'd had an aide show her to earlier in the day. With long raking strides he set off after her.

Jayne collapsed into the leather chair behind Tariq's desk. Her first reaction was to hop onto the Internet, to see if Helen was still awake. She felt lonely and isolated and incredibly homesick. She wanted her family, she wanted to go home, to leave this inhospitable country that had never brought her anything but pain.

The soft sound of the door closing brought the first hint that she was no longer alone.

"What did Ali say to make you leave?" An implacable anger glowed in Tariq's eyes.

"It doesn't matter." Ali had been his usual obnoxious self. He'd taunted her by saying that had his daughter married Tariq, she would have done her duty, borne him fine sons and done him proud as a hostess. She'd been stupid to let Ali get to her. Jayne shook her head, suddenly overwhelmingly aware of the heat of Tariq's body behind her, the soft hiss of his breath beside her ear as he leaned forward. Instantly, nerves started to churn in her belly. She lifted her hand from the mouse and spun the leather office chair around. Only to find herself face-to-face with Tariq. This close his eyes had the appearance of molten gold. Ensnaring her. Trapping her in the rich heat.

"It matters. You are my wife."

She held his knee-weakening gaze. "Not for long."

"For at least a month. And for that month I expect my countrymen to treat you with the respect that you deserve."

"The respect I deserve because I am your woman? Or the respect that I deserve in my own right?"

"Is there a difference?" He lifted his hand to touch her cheek. "I touch this skin. It belongs to my wife and it belongs to Jayne, too. They are one and the same."

"Jayne Jones is not your possession."

He didn't answer. His finger trailed down, across her lips, sensitising the soft skin.

"I should go," she whispered against his finger.

"I don't think so."

She stared at him, her breathing quickening, tingles of apprehension mingled with excitement shivered down her spine. Trouble.

"You're aware of me. Your body recognizes me."

"That doesn't mean you own me."

"My body responds to you, too. Even though I resist it. You own me every bit as much as I own you." Taking her hands, he pulled her out of the chair, against the hard, muscled length of his body. Instantly, she felt the hardness of his arousal against her stomach.

"I am leaving."

"Too late." His head swooped down, his mouth slanting across hers.

Heat and light and emotion scorched Jayne as his mouth met hers. All rational thought left Jayne as she parted her lips and started to kiss her husband back.

Four

All thoughts of her family, her sister, her nieces, flew away as Tariq's mouth plundered hers. His kiss was uncompromising and the flare of heat that started deep in her stomach took her by surprise.

It had been a long time.

Too long, since she'd last felt this intensity of emotion.

As his hand threaded through her hair at the back of her neck, his fingers brushed the sensitive skin of her nape and a frisson of delight ran through her. Tariq knew exactly where to touch…to arouse her, to turn her. The fingertips now moving in little circles sent shivers through her and his lips demanded a response.

Jayne gave a little gasp, taken aback by the pent up passion that Tariq had unleashed. Instantly he pressed closer, his tongue stroking into her mouth, tasting her, slower now, languidly, as if he could never get enough.

With a groan she reached up, locking her arms around his neck, conscious of her breasts growing taut and tender as her body melted against him. She felt like a flower blooming, unfurling, under the heat of the sun. Tariq's hands shifted against the back of her head, cradling her, bringing her closer still. She was sharply, disconcertingly aware of the tips of her breasts hardening under the loose fabric of the caftan, of the brush of his chest against the taut mounds.

Then, as suddenly as it had begun, the kiss was over.

The chill that followed the wave of heat shocked her. Jayne shivered with regret. Until those drive-me-crazy hands moved again, tilting her head, and his lips landed on the soft, exposed skin of her neck. A guttural sound exploded from her. She closed her eyes and let her head fall back, giving herself up to his touch, to the sheer indescribable delight. The fingers spearing through her hair released a fresh wave of shivers. And her body felt soft and pliable, boneless with want.

His teeth scraped her skin, his tongue followed, and Jayne gasped again. His mouth closed on the sensitive area beneath her ear…a trail of hot kisses, then a long stroke of his tongue set her on edge. Jayne waited…every nerve ending quivering…eager for what would come next.

In some distant space of her mind, she was half-aware of his hands leaving her hair, sliding over her shoulders, down her back, and she arched like a cat about to be stroked.

But when she felt his fingers stop, linger, and her bra strap give under the fabric of the caftan, she tensed, jolted by reality.

What was she doing?

She should not be allowing Tariq to kiss her like this. Ali's words echoed hollowly in her head. Tariq needed a wife who would do her duty…and that woman was not her. So what on earth was she doing responding to her soon-to-be-ex like this? She couldn't jeopardise her newly planned life simply because Tariq still turned her on.

She'd almost left it too late. Jenna heard the rasp of a zipper, felt the caftan give.

"No!"

Tariq's hands stilled. "What do you mean 'No'? You are my wife!"

"No!" She shuddered. She couldn't survive the half world, the dry wasteland that had been her marriage. "I'll never be your wife again, Tariq. Our marriage is over." She wanted a divorce, to put Tariq and her marriage behind her and move on.

She tore out of his arms, ducked under his arm, and put half the length of the room between them. "I don't want this."

"Liar." His voice was flat, his face expressionless. The light in the golden eyes had been extinguished. "You responded to me."

He was right. She'd been far too…engaged. But she couldn't afford to let him know that. So she looked away. "Maybe I'd have responded to any attractive man."

"Any man?" It was a soft snarl, dangerous. "Not only me? So where does that leave the blond man who waits for you back home in Auckland, my faithless, lying wife?"

She stared at him blankly.

"Neil Woodruffe," he said silkily. "Or had you forgotten all about the poor bastard you are holding on a string?"

"How do you know about Neil?" Neil had asked her out several times over the past months. Lately he'd taken to visiting her apartment on flimsy excuses. She'd humoured him, inviting him in. But how did Tariq know about Neil? A sick tightness gripped Jayne. One glance at Tariq's face confirmed her suspicious. "You're having me watched."

He didn't deny it.

"That's disgusting." The words burst from her. She *hated* the thought that he was spying on her. "Does it make you feel powerful to follow the details of my life? That's sick!"

"I employed a detective when you initiated contact. You should remember that I have always believed information is key to any negotiation." He gave her a tight smile.

Jayne's heart thumped in her chest, so loudly that she feared he might hear. "Your lack of trust is the reason why I don't want to be married to you anymore."

"Do you blame me?" His mouth tightened. "No, don't answer that, there's no point in rehashing the past. Our marriage is over. In a month you will have your divorce, maybe sooner."

The next day Tariq stormed down the corridor to his father's apartments, his white *thobe* billowing behind him, still seething about how Jayne had managed to put him on the back foot the night before. Why was he thinking about her, when he had this whole disaster with Mahood and Ali to worry about…and he'd just been summoned to his father's side. Had the end come?

With his father dead, Jayne would get her divorce sooner than she'd hoped.

There would be no reason to keep her in Zayed.

The palace guard leapt to attention as he swept past. "His Excellency is awake?" he asked the male nurse who was filling out a clipboard in the antechamber.

"Not only am I awake—I'm refusing to take the drugs,

which is why they have called you." The voice was thin and thready, but the eyes that met Tariq's as he rushed into the bedchamber, with the nurse at his heels, held a hint of the old fire.

"Leave us," Tariq commanded the nurse. Retreating with a respectful bow, the nurse closed the door.

"Father." Tariq sank to one knee beside the bed. "You must take the morphine, it will help the pain."

"I am feeling much better. The confusion and dizzy head is less now that I abandon the medicine." His father's hand rested on top of Tariq's head. Gone was the solid weight that had stroked his hair as a child. No longer the hand of a ruler feared and revered by his subjects, but the wavering touch of a dying man. Tariq swallowed the hot thickness in his throat.

"Hadi al Ebrahim has been to see me." Tariq's head rose as his father spoke. "He tells me the sheikhah has returned."

Hadi was one of his father's most trusted aides. Tariq nodded. "She came to see you but you were—" *drugged* "—sleeping." He watched his father carefully, unsure of what to say next. A couple of months ago, soon after the terrible diagnosis, Tariq had heard rumours that his father had sent Hadi on a mission to Sheikh Karim—a mission that he was not prepared to confront his father about now that he was dying. Instead he'd obliquely mentioned to his father that in terms of his marriage contract with Jayne he could take only one wife at a time. His father had looked fit to burst, calling Tariq a foolish monkey. Tariq certainly hadn't expected his father to be overjoyed by Jayne's return. But, for his father to die in peace, he needed to convince his father that marriage to Jayne was what he, Tariq, wanted more than anything on earth….

"Good. It is time that your wife resumes her position at your side."

Tariq's mouth fell open. While he was aware that his father wanted him contently married before he died, he'd anticipated a little more resistance. Especially as his father had evidently had other plans.

"Hadi is worried," the Emir said. "He says that Ali and Mahood can make a lot of trouble for Karim—and for you."

Tariq shrugged. "I'm sorry to say this, Father, but their trouble causing is not new." And if Hadi had been acting as a go-between to broker a marriage between Tariq and Sheikh Karim's half sister, then Hadi would have even more cause for concern.

"But this time they have angered Karim, you need to placate him, we cannot afford to have an angry neighbouring ruler—especially not one as powerful as the sheikh of Bashir. What will happen to our oil interests in Bashir if we are in conflict with each other?"

"I know. I have been in touch." Sheikh Karim had laid the blame squarely at Ali and Mahood's feet, saying they illicitly grazed herds of livestock over the border and had appropriated animals that did not belong to them. Karim had confiscated the whole herd the next time the animals had returned and impounded them.

Tariq gave a sharp sigh. "I will go—" He broke off and closed his eyes. What if his father died while he was gone? What if he missed these precious last days because of the stupidity and stubbornness of Ali and Mahood?

"When? You cannot wait."

Tormented, Tariq opened his eyes and looked into the dark orbs close to his own. Eyes that in the past had been filled with love…anger…disappointment…and now held only a stoic acceptance.

No, he wanted to yell. *Fight it.* Don't die.

Don't leave me.

Alone.

"You can't wait, my son. You must go. Now."

Silently Tariq shook his head. His father's hands were thin, the purple veins showing through the wrinkled skin. The skin that hung over his face showed a waxen cast…like a death mask, the eyes deeply sunken in the sockets.

"I order you." It was a command, gasped out by a man used to being obeyed.

Tariq stiffened. He knew that his father would read his refusal in his eyes. He would not go. He could not leave his father. Not so near the end.

"Please."

This time it was a plea. Tariq stared at the man who had never begged for anything in his life. The man that no one disobeyed.

"What if…" Tariq swallowed the words, unable to finish the thought.

But his father knew. "What if I die? *Inshallah.* It will not happen yet, I am feeling a lot better. But you cannot hover around waiting for that hour like a vulture in the noonday sky. You have a destiny…and Zayed needs you."

Tariq started to answer back.

"Do not argue with your father. I am an old, sick man." The bloodless lips curved into a ghost of a smile. "And by Allah, this will be the last task I ask of you, I promise that. Make peace with Karim and I will ask no more."

"He will expect an apology."

His father nodded.

"I will have to put something in it for him…land or oil leases."

His father nodded again.

"I will go tomorrow."

"Take your wife with you."

"What?" On his way to the door, Tariq stopped and stared at his father in disbelief. He'd already planned to take Jayne with him, in order to make it doubly clear to Karim that he was not in the market for a wife. Not even for Karim's ever-so-suitable half sister. But he'd never expected his father to suggest the same. He'd thought his father wanted the…merger…with Karim. It would've been convenient for all concerned. And for the two oil-rich desert countries.

"He needs to accept your wife…as I have. To know there will be no marriage between you and his sister."

There, it was out in the open.

So the rumours were true. His father had tried to broker a new marriage for him. But hearing that Tariq could only take one wife—a wife he had not chosen to divorce—must have dissuaded him from meddling further.

A gnarled hand reached out from the bed. "My son, do not repeat my mistakes with your own wife."

Crossing the room in one stride, Tariq closed his hands around the thin bones. "What do you mean, Father?"

For a while the Emir did not answer. Finally he said. "I am tired. Never forget, I am proud of you, my son. Now I need the morphine."

Tariq's hand went to the bell. The nurse arrived in a rush. The drug was administered, and his father's eyes closed.

Tariq lingered a few minutes, a deep sense of loss swarming through him. What had his father been about to reveal? Finally he leant over to kiss the wrinkled brow. In his heart he feared this was the last time he might see his father alive.

The notion shook him to his soul.

* * *

Jayne was sitting at the stone table in the walled arbour beside the fountain, catching a little morning sun and writing out postcards to Samantha and Amy when the sound of Tariq's footsteps clattered on the stone stairs.

"I have been to see my father," Tariq announced, his eyes unreadable.

He dominated the comforting enclosed space of the arbour. His height, his presence, the scent of the citrusy cologne that clung to his skin all overwhelmed Jayne. She set her pen down. "You talked about your mother?"

"No!" His answer was uncompromising. "You may have heard that there is trouble brewing between Ali and Mahood and Sheikh Karim al Bashir?"

She nodded. It would've been difficult not to have heard the rumours that flew around the palace, or the speculation about how Tariq would react. The Emir was dying. Would he placate his father's oldest friends? Or would he make amends to the furious Karim?

"Zayed must avoid a war with Sheikh Karim at all costs."

Her brow creased, trying to remember what she'd heard. "He's the ruler of a neighbouring sheikhdom, right?"

"Yes. We have many alliances—particularly over oil. We can't afford to antagonise him."

"Ali and Mahood are more trouble than they are worth," she said daringly.

"Mahood and Ali are my father's closest friends. Like brothers to him. I have to respect that bond."

Jayne said nothing. His reply left no room for argument. He would put up with Mahood and Ali and all their guile for his love of his father.

"The trip to the desert town of Aziz should take no longer than three days. I plan to travel swiftly."

He must fear that his father would die in his absence. Her heart squeezed at the sight of the pain etched into his features as he towered over her.

"What about—" *His father.* She broke off, her heart going out to Tariq. What if his father did die while he was gone? What if he left to sort out Ali and Mahood's skirmishes and never saw his father again? As much as she loathed Sheik Rashid, Tariq loved his father.

"What about you? Or what about the divorce that you desire so highly?" His mouth curled into an unpleasant smile. "Your first thought is about yourself."

It was so unfair! But her heart sank at the derision in his eyes, and for the first time she felt relief that she would be staying in the palace. Being surrounded by hostile aides was better than accompanying Tariq in this mood. "I have to think about me," she fired back. "No one else does. You've brought me all the way across the world to cool my heels and await your return and twiddle my thumbs. To waste my time. I have things I want to do." Like start her new course…and have a date with Neil…and start a new life, out from under Tariq's shadow. "What if there are delays and this all takes more than three days? Does that mean you will expect me to stay longer?"

The bubbling of the water in the fountain was the only sound that broke the silence. But the soothing sound did nothing to comfort her as she waited for his reply.

At last he spoke and his eyes were hard. "I won't leave my father for as long as a week. Not when he is so near the end. Nor will I be leaving you to cool your heels, *habiibtii.* You will be coming with me. Be ready to leave by daybreak."

* * *

The courtyard behind the palace was already bustling when Jayne got there the following morning.

Tariq was waiting beside a lone white SUV, clad in a *thobe* with a *ghutra* tied with two rounds of black cord around his head. The SUV had already been packed high with provisions. In the back, beside their bags, Jayne spotted a *kafas,* a cage with holes to allow circulation, holding Noor along with large storage bottles of water—a sobering reminder of exactly how remote their destination was.

Jayne slowed to a halt in front of Tariq. "Is this it?"

He raised an eyebrow. "You were expecting camels?"

Not camels. Anyway, the white SUV was the modern equivalent of the white stallion for a desert traveller. But she'd expected some sort of entourage. Tariq never went anywhere alone. Bodyguards. Aides. A veritable army accompanied him. "When we travelled before—"

"Last time I organised camels because that's what you wanted."

She gave up. They were talking at cross purposes. He was referring to the trip they'd made in the first few months after their return to Zayed not long after their marriage in London. He'd taken her into the desert—by camel. They'd camped out under velvet skies studded with stars as bright as diamonds.

"You expected the fantasy," he was saying, his eyes intent. "A desert romance. That excursion was supposed to be romantic—to make up for the honeymoon I'd never given you."

She clambered into the vehicle and muttered dismissively, "Another mirage."

"What do you mean?" He leaned in through the doorway, his brows fierce.

She shrugged, reluctant to get into a skirmish, and stared through the windshield determined not to look at him. "Don't worry about it. It's nothing."

"When a woman says 'It's nothing' only a fool believes her."

Jayne remained mute, pressing her lips firmly together.

She sensed him watching her. After a long moment he sighed and shut the door before walking around the front of the vehicle to hop in beside her. A flick of his wrist and the vehicle roared to life. Jayne put her head back on the headrest and closed her eyes.

Their desert romance had been nothing more than a mirage. Even that belated honeymoon had been cut short. After only two days a helicopter had landed where they were camped. Tariq had been summoned back to the palace. During the flight back he'd apologised. Promised that there'd be other times.

And Jayne had been left wondering if it had been another instance of the long hand of the Emir acting to destroy their marriage.

When she'd been taken ill with a violent stomach bug the next day, she hated everything in the desert…and Zayed.

But that was in the past.

In the end, the Emir had won.

Their entire marriage had been a mirage.

Now she'd finally made herself a new life. A real life. And she was ready to move on. Find an ordinary man with whom to create a real marriage with real children.

Turning her head, Jayne focused on the passing landscape. The morning was lovely. A smattering of clouds meant that the heat had lost the edge common even in the winter months.

"It's hot," she said a while later, more to break the throbbing silence than because the heat worried her.

"Tonight will be cool in the desert." His hand flicked a dial, and a blast of cold air swirled around her. "Better?"

She stared at the lean hands on the steering wheel, and a bolt of emotion shot through her. No, it wasn't better. The cold air did nothing to alleviate her inner tension. She swallowed. "Yes," she said finally. "It's cooler."

A sideways glance revealed a hard, hawkish profile. The white *ghutra* should have softened his jagged profile; instead it added to the mystique and ruthlessness of the man. Her gaze lingered on the black *agal*—the cords that wound twice around his headdress and hung down his back. Beside his mouth, the deep, scored lines showed the strain he was under. Tariq must be terribly worried about his father…and then there was this situation that Ali and Mahood had created. She had to remember that if she felt tense, he was under infinitely more stress. Finally she turned her head away and tipped her head back again, closing her eyes, and tried to doze.

Jayne woke suddenly to find that several hours had passed and she was chilled. The desert sun had vanished and a white blanket of cloud stretched across the sky. The air-conditioning was chilly enough to have Jayne reaching into her bag for a lightweight merino cardigan.

"Cold?" Tariq fiddled with the air-conditioning controls, and the rush of cool air slowed.

"A little. Despite the heat that is probably out there." She gestured to the desert that stretched out, bleak and inhospitable, in every direction.

"The cloud cover makes today cooler than normal." Tariq dipped his head and glanced up through the windshield. "I don't like the look of them, they've been gathering over the last hour." He slowed and examined a gadget that had to be a GPS.

Four-wheel-drive. GPS. What was she worried about? This was the twenty-first century. The desert was not as alien and threatening as she imagined. She was overreacting, allowing her dislike and resentment of Zayed to get to her. Jayne laughed. "Rain? Little chance of that out here."

"The desert does get storms, not often but they happen. They can be devastating because the desert does not absorb the water. So it gathers on the surface until there is sufficient for floods."

"Floods?" Jayne stared at the barren landscape and her apprehension crept back. Just enough to make prickles rise at her the base of her neck. "Hard to imagine."

"Believe it. As much as water brings life, rain can wreak havoc."

"Will we be able to reach Aziz before the rain comes?"

"Maybe. If it comes at all. The clouds may dissipate— not uncommon."

"That would be a relief." The prospect of a desert storm did not thrill Jayne. She stared out of the window at the clouds, then at the expanse of stony ground that stretched without end to the horizon. It gave the desert a foreboding feeling, even greater than it already possessed, and Jayne shivered.

Another hour passed. They'd stopped briefly to eat pita rounds filled with shredded lamb and lettuce and tomato and drink bottles of mineral water, before setting off again. Since the meal, Tariq had been silent, but Jayne thought that they'd picked up speed. The banks of cloud had been rolling, piling high into stacks that made Jayne's insides twist.

"I hate this place." Jayne's tension spilled over. "I really do."

"I know." Tariq's voice held a bleak quality that made Jayne give him a quick glance.

"You shouldn't have made me come back to Zayed."

"I needed you."

Her heart missed a beat. In the past she would have killed for an admission like that. But Tariq had been more focused on his father, on the good of Zayed than on her. She'd been lonely, her heart bruised by his lack of care.

"To convince your father that you will be settled after his death?"

"In my country it is believed if a man has given all his children in marriage through the course of his lifetime, then he has successfully fulfilled the duty of his life. Our marriage is not what my father considers a real marriage, so he considers that he has failed to fulfill the duty of his life. He wants me to be happily married. He believes it is time for me to have a family, children." Tariq sighed. "He's even tried to use a go-between to offer a bride price…he's been plotting to find me a second wife."

Second wife. She should've expected this. But still her heart plummeted at the news. Tariq with a family. With children. Once upon a time that had been her dream. "He can't do that," she said. "Our marriage contract—"

"Forbids that. I know. And I have advised my father that we added a clause that I may not marry another woman while married to you."

Jayne had insisted on it. Even young and desperately in love, she hadn't been able to overcome her greatest fear: that one day her gorgeous Zayedi husband would find a more beautiful, more accomplished wife and wish to marry a second time. Not even the status of being the senior wife would have made up for that. She'd wanted to be his only love. Forever.

Sadly, she'd never considered requesting a clause that allowed her to divorce her husband without his consent. If she had, she'd never have needed to return to Zayed. Back then, lighthearted with love, she'd thought that her marriage would last longer than the sands of the desert.

"Your father couldn't have been pleased." Jayne guessed that was an understatement. The Emir would've been enraged. Why hadn't he demanded that Tariq divorce her?

Immediately.

"No, he wasn't." Tariq's reply held a certain wryness. "But at least it appeared to put a stop to his quest to find me a second wife although certain…complications…were caused by his enthusiastic matchmaking."

"Serves him right! He never approved of our marriage. So don't expect me to be a hypocrite and stay for the funeral after he—" she swallowed "—dies."

"Why would I want you to stay for my father's funeral?" Tariq looked away from the road ahead. The eyes that met hers were full of turmoil. "You're not—"

The ring of a cell phone rent the air, interrupting what he'd been about to say. He hit the button where the phone rested in its housing on the dashboard. "Yes?" Tariq demanded tersely.

Jayne was relieved. There had been something in his eyes…

She suspected she wasn't ready to hear what he'd wanted to say. Not here stuck out in the middle of this inhospitable terrain with nowhere to run.

When he ended the call, he said, "There is concern about the weather. We will stop at a Bedu camp not far from here to take shelter from the cloudburst that the meteorologists are predicting."

Five

As they approached the Bedouin camp, Jayne stared with interest at the tents that nestled at the base of a rocky rise.

"These are Bedu tribal lands," Tariq told her as he headed the SUV for a huddle of tents. "You can't see it clearly from here, but on the other side of the ridge there is a village with a school and a clinic, and in the surrounding area efforts are being made at de-desertification."

"What do you mean?" Jayne turned to look at him and couldn't help noticing how he speeded up his speech, how his eyes sparkled as he spoke. He loved the desert and its people as much as she hated it.

"There are olive groves planted in the desert."

"But who looks after them?" She stared at their surroundings. "Aren't the Bedu nomads, always on the move?"

"In the past, yes, but things change...although some still follow the old ways, others are setting down roots."

Jayne gestured to the array of tents. "Some of those tents are huge. But are you saying there are brick-and-mortar dwellings?"

"Yes, over the rise."

"I think I prefer the idea of tents. I always wanted to stay in a Bedouin camp," she said a little dreamily.

"I remember." He gave a laugh.

"But we didn't find a Bedouin tent that time…although I did get to ride into the desert on a camel and camp in the tent you put up." Jayne thought back to that disastrous trip.

Seconds later Tariq pulled up to where a group of men sat outside in the thin shade of a tamarisk tree playing cards. They looked up. All play stopped.

One of the men jumped to his feet and came to shake Tariq's hand. "Excellency, we did not know you were visiting. We welcome you."

Tariq flung an arm to the overcast sky. "The weather has forced us on you, and we would be grateful for your hospitality for a night."

"Only a pleasure, Excellency. You are welcome for more than one miserable night. My residence is not far from here. It is new and you will not lack for luxury."

A smile played around Tariq's mouth. "I thank you for your offer. But the sheikhah has a fancy to stay in a tent—if that is not too much for us to ask."

The headman, whom Tariq introduced as Ghayth, looked at Jayne as if she were touched by the moon, then glanced at the sky. "But, Excellency, if the rain comes, the area outside the tent will be a mudbath."

Tariq raised an eyebrow at Jayne. "The tents themselves won't leak, they're constructed to withstand the elements, sun, wind, sandstorms. But are you sure you wouldn't rather stay under a solid roof?"

"As long as it's not going to cause problems for our hosts or uncomfortable flooding for you if the rains come, I'd rather stay in a Bedouin tent. It sounds like an experience of a lifetime." She was touched that he was trying to accommodate her quirky dreams, rather than practicalities. She gave him a small smile. "Thank you, Tariq."

The tent to which they were led was far larger than she had expected—and far more luxurious than the shelters on the outskirts of the encampment. Inside it was divided with drapes into two separate areas.

"This is the meeting area," Tariq said, waving to the large space around them furnished with several squat square stools covered with woven fabric and a long divan covered with similar material. In the corner stood a round table with four chairs set around it, and the walls and floors were covered with beautifully woven rugs. "Traditionally the curtained-off area is where the women prepare food in the day and where the family sleeps at night. But this tent is more ornate, probably kept for visiting dignitaries, that's why there are no cooking arrangements. The de-desertification program has been attracting a lot of interest—even from the UN."

"Oh." Jayne took in the rugs, the drapes that hung from the roof. "It's certainly not quite as modest as I expected."

Tariq pulled back the drapes to reveal a couple of broad low divans draped with rugs. The sleeping quarters. Instantly a subtle tension invaded the room.

"I think I need a wash," Jayne said, suddenly eager to get out of the tent she'd been so keen to experience. She had a feeling that she was going to be very pleased that the tent was a lot more spacious than she'd anticipated. Perhaps it would've been wiser to have accepted the offer of a stay in Ghayth's house…at least she would've had her own bedroom.

"You can bathe later," Tariq said, "after dinner. For now, use the water in the pitcher on the table to freshen up. Our hosts will be here shortly with our bags. Then we need to see that Noor has been fed and bedded down."

An hour later the clouds, while still ominous, seemed to have lifted a little. They no longer sagged with moisture overhead. Ghayth, the headman, met Jayne and Tariq as they headed back from feeding Noor, with an offer to show Jayne the nearby village.

Within minutes they'd piled into their host's very battered four-wheel drive, with the two salukis in the back, and roared down the dirt road that cut across the stony terrain. Tariq sat up front beside Ghayth, and Jayne sat beside his senior wife, Matra, whose name meant "pot that catches the rain," Jayne discovered as they drove past the olive groves surrounded by desert sand that Tariq had told her about.

From the pointing and the rapid questions he fired at their host, Jayne realised that Tariq was a lot more involved in the program than she'd suspected.

A little way on they turned down a track and the village came into view. A group of children were huddled around a bicycle that leaned against a scrawny tree and they all turned to stare curiously at the approaching vehicle.

Once they had stopped, Jayne descended from the vehicle and followed the men. Carpets in shades of ruby, garnet and topaz were spread out in the patchy sunlight, and a dozen or more women sat around weaving. Jayne caught her breath at vivid designs and colours. "They are beautiful."

One of the women gave her a gentle smile.

"How long does it take you to make such a rug?" Jayne asked, bending down to touch the design.

The woman looked at the men, a frown pleating her forehead.

"She does not speak any English," Tariq said, and rattled off in Arabic. The woman nodded and said something. "She says it depends on how many women are working on the design," Tariq translated.

"They must do well out of such rugs. The craftsmanship is wonderful."

"Not yet. The project has only been going for a couple of years. It's supposed to be self-driven by the village women, so it has taken some time for the women to get it off the ground."

"That's heartbreaking. The rugs are so amazing. I can think of people in Auckland who would pay a fortune for such finery." She thought of Neil, of his home in Remuera with the collection of fine furniture and antique books.

"There is no question of their talent, or their entrepreneurial skills. But some of the women are reticent. They are used to the men running things. But they are insistent that this is their project. They've had a lot to learn. Accounts. Running a business. Distribution."

"And a lot of us can't read or write, which makes it much harder," Matra said softly from behind Jayne's shoulder.

Jayne knew she shouldn't be surprised. But somehow she was. "I thought Zayed was progressive country, that a lot of the wealth from the oil fields is poured into education and development."

"It is," Tariq said levelly, and Jayne realised he'd taken her words as criticism. "But there are a lot of nomadic tribes in Zayed, too."

"And some of us are too old to learn," Matra said, her expression showing that it took a lot of bravery to converse with Tariq.

Jayne considered her. "No one is ever too old to learn."

The daylight waned quickly as they returned to the camp. Night fell like a cloak over the desert, and Jayne found herself shivering as the temperature plummeted. Dark clouds swarmed overhead, but the rain that had threatened did not come, much to the glee of their hosts.

The Bedu had prepared an outdoor feast to celebrate their arrival. A fire had been lit and everyone sat around the flames.

An hour later Jayne sat back replete, and weariness seeped through her. She watched as the men seated around the fire clamoured for Tariq's attention. He listened, nodded, spoke a few words, then turned to the next person.

Matra came toward her carrying a copper pot with a long spout and murmured something Jayne did not understand. So she smiled and spread her hands helplessly.

"What is that?"

Before Matra could reply, Tariq was at her side. "Matra is offering you coffee."

Jayne nodded enthusiastically. "Coffee would be lovely."

Matra put the coffeepot down and disappeared.

"It's Bedu coffee," Tariq warned. "Strong and bitter. The coffee beans are roasted on a long shovel and then ground with a mortar before being brewed for several hours."

The other woman returned with a tray of tiny handleless cups and filled them from the coffeepot and handed one to

Jayne who eyed the greenish-brown liquid with suspicion. "It's not as dark as normal coffee."

"That's the cardamom. You drink the whole cup down in one sip."

"O-kay." Jayne took a deep breath and gulped, then almost choked as the bitterness hit her throat. "At least these cups only hold a sip or two," she murmured. "Otherwise I might have to develop a coffee allergy."

Tariq threw his head back and laughed. Jayne stared. How long had it been since he had laughed like that? When she'd first known him, his infectious laughter, his joie de vivre, had been one of the first things to attract her. Tariq had loved life—and lived it joyously.

She hadn't realised how much she had missed his good humour. Until now.

Matra was back offering the tray again. Tariq took another cup and smiled at the woman, who lowered her eyes. Sucking in a deep breath, Jayne reached for another cup.

"How am I going to drink this?"

"Slowly," Tariq responded, but his eyes danced.

She took a tiny sip and pulled a surreptitious face.

"Here, give it to me."

"It's okay, I don't want to be rude."

His hand closed around hers. He brought the cup up to his mouth. Under the pressure of his hand, she tipped the cup. He sipped. This close the gold eyes gleamed like burnished bronze. Caught in the snare of his gaze, she stared at him, suddenly breathless.

His lips lifted off the rim of the minute cup. "There is one last sip. For you."

His hands still cupping hers, she placed her lips against the opposite rim from where he had drunk. The cup tilted. She drank.

"How does it taste now?" His voice was husky. "Still bitter?"

She licked her lips clean of the last smears of coffee. As her tongue tip skimmed across her bottom lip, his eyes flared to the colour of midnight. The shock of the change from gold to dark sent a bolt of sensation through her.

She hurriedly retracted her tongue, swallowed and realised that the bitter taste had gone. All that remained was the distinctive flavour of cardamom. "No, not bitter."

How had this happened?

How had she become so aware of him standing so close to her, to his hand still grasping hers?

Jayne pulled away…and found Matra at her elbow. Jayne looked at the cups of coffee, glanced at Tariq and knew he, too, was supremely conscious of the heat that sizzled between them.

"Accepting a third cup means that you consider yourself one of the family. If you deliberately refuse this cup…it will be considered rude," he murmured softly.

Quickly she nodded to Marta. And so did Tariq. Following his lead, she tossed it back, trying very hard not to grimace and set the empty cup on the tray.

"Now you can refuse the next cup. Because after three cups it is considered rude to take another."

"Thank goodness," she murmured.

"You did fine. Come, it is time to say good-night."

A fine quivering sensation started deep in her stomach as they walked across the shadowed camp to their tent, the indigo night sky arching overhead. Jayne was aware of the darkness that stretched into the desert beyond their tent. The vast emptiness that surrounded them, broken only by the soft conversation of the Bedouin still gathered around the fire.

Their tent glowed inside, the soft light of candles diffusing against the drapes in a warm pattern.

"In the sleeping area there is a bath ready for you," Tariq said. "Matra arranged it."

"Oh." Jayne felt suddenly breathless. "I had thought there might be a washroom nearby."

"There is—with communal baths. No doubt Matra thought you would prefer to bathe in private."

Private?

With Tariq here?

Dragging her feet, Jayne made her way to where Tariq had pointed. A steaming bath waited, with a high back and a curved lip to rest her head on. After the drive and the long day, it looked too welcoming to refuse. Quickly she shucked off her clothes and stepped in, sinking down into the hot water. Shivers broke across her skin as ripples of heat enfolded her.

She tried to relax. But couldn't. Not with Tariq standing on the other side of that filmy drape.

Tariq lay sprawled across the divan in the outer compartment and listened to the soft lap of the water every time Jayne moved.

This was Jayne. The wife he'd banished. He shut his eyes, trying to block out the tantalising sounds. But then he'd hear it again. Slap, slap. He could visualise her. Naked. In the tub less than ten metres away. Her long hair secured on top of her head with a rubber band, her cheeks flushed from the steam.

No. He couldn't think about this. The kiss the other night at the state dinner had been an aberration. A mistake caused by the protectiveness aroused by the attack on Jayne in the city—and his reaction to the pain in her eyes at whatever cruel taunts Ali had made. The kiss was not to be repeated. It had been inspired by soft-hearted pity, his protective instincts. Nothing more.

He certainly couldn't *want* his wife. Not anymore. Not after—

Slap, slap.

She must be moving, causing the water to ripple. He couldn't bear it! "Do you need something?"

"No, no. I'm fine."

At last there was silence.

He told himself that it was relief that pooled in his stomach, that he wasn't thinking about the way her dark eyes had laughed up into his when he'd sipped from her coffee cup. He wasn't imagining her pale, soft skin slick with water; or the sweet curve of her breast, the dark cherry nipples that he'd loved to taste.

But as his body started to harden, he knew he lied.

The discovery was devastating.

"Tariq?"

At her call he was instantly on his feet.

"Don't come in," she said hastily.

He dared not. "I won't." It came out thick and muffled, like something was strangling him. He cleared his throat and tried again. "What do you want?"

What do you want? He shut his eyes and clenched his hands into fists as his words echoed in the intimacy of the tent.

"Some soap, please."

"How am I supposed to give you soap if I can't come in?"

"I don't know." Her voice was so soft he had to strain his ears to hear. "I suppose I could do without it."

"You'll feel better if you're properly washed."

"I suppose."

Tariq spied the soap. On the table in the corner, on top of a thick white towel. A shower cap lay beside it—and a bottle of shampoo.

"Would you like shampoo, too?"

"Yes, please, if it isn't too much trouble."

"No trouble." And wished that were true. He gathered up the bar of soap, the shampoo and the towel. Raising his voice, he said, "So how am I supposed to get this to you without stepping behind the curtain?"

"Close your eyes. Approach one step at a time. I'll tell you when you can drop them."

He strode to the curtain, shut his eyes, hauled in a deep breath that shuddered to the bottom of his chest and pushed the drape aside.

"I'm here."

A careful step in the direction of her voice. And another. She moved. He heard the lap of the water and prickles of arousal gathered in his groin. He thanked Allah for the towel that hid that evidence of his desire for her.

Only a small distance away, Jayne was naked.

Don't think about it.

Don't look.

How could he not? It had been too long since he'd seen those full breasts with the crimson tips and the tight stomach, below which lay the lush dark curls that…

Desire shafted through him, making him rock hard.

He fought the temptation to look.

And won.

Quickly he took another step. The scent of jasmine bath oil surrounded him, pungent, sensual.

"Stop!"

He obeyed, unbearably aroused by the hot steamy scent of the perfumed water, the thought that she lay naked less than an arm's length from him and the fact that he was performing personal, intimate chores at her command.

"Hold the soap and the shampoo out."

Like an automaton, he found his arms extending. The towel slithered down, landing at his feet. He heard the water swirl, knew she must be sitting up, that her breasts would be moving, glistening with moisture. He bit back a groan, and squeezed his eyes more tightly shut, leashing the urge to look.

"You can let them go."

Only then did he realise that he was clutching the toiletries so tightly that the shampoo bottle had buckled under the force. Jayne's hands, hot and wet from the water, reached for his. His eyes still closed, he bit back a groan, as her fingers slid wetly against his.

"I've got the bottle, let go!"

Hastily he released the toiletries. The shampoo bottle slid into her grip while the soap splashed into the bath. A moment later he heard the sensual lap of water against her skin.

Unable to resist, he opened his eyes.

The shampoo bottle sat on the lip of the bath. Jayne was leaning forward, both hands searching the water for the soap. From this angle, the beautiful breasts he remembered were hidden, and her back was pale and smooth and sleek under the lamplight. Her hair was piled on top of her head in a shining mass, and her nape was exposed.

Even conscious that she'd hate to know that he'd looked at her, that what he was doing was forbidden and wrong, Tariq couldn't stop staring at the wife who wanted nothing more than to be rid of him. Contrarily he itched to lean forward and place his lips against her nape, to stroke her wet back, dip his hands forward into the water and cup her breasts in his hands.

By Zayed, what was he doing? He would never take her back. What she'd done was too terrible to ever forgive…or forget.

He swung away. Grabbing a towel and a bar of soap off the table in the outer area, Tariq charged out the tent. Away from temptation. From ruination. By the time he returned after a long, ice-cold shower in the communal washrooms, Jayne was asleep.

She lay on her side, her hands pressed together under her cheek, looking barely a day older than when he'd first run into her in the Tate Gallery.

Picking up a woven angora rug, Tariq placed the extra layer over her, to protect her from the desert night chill. Then he sank down onto the wide divan beside her. He stroked the long strands of hair away from her face and stared at the alabaster skin, the red lips that had called for his kisses from the first moment he'd laid eyes on her, when she'd looked up at him, her mouth a startled *O*.

He fought the urge to kiss that terribly tempting mouth. His hands trembled a little as he gave her hair a last stroke. It shattered him that he still wanted his wife.

Despite what she had done.

Jayne awoke early the next morning. The tent was in darkness and there was no sign of Tariq. She rose, found the matches on the table in the outer area and lit a tall candle. Then she washed her face quickly using the bowl and cold water in the pitcher on the table in the outer compartment of the tent. And wondered where Tariq had gone.

Holding the candle high, Jayne returned to the sleep section and paused as she noticed the imprint of a bigger, heavier body on the divan beside where she had lain. Tariq must've slept beside her all night long. Heat uncurled in her stomach at the thought of him lying close beside her. And she hadn't even known.

Probably better so. She would've had to send him away.

Setting the candle down, she hunted through her bag for a pair of lightweight dark trousers with narrow-cut legs and a shift dress in a leopard print to wear over the top. By now the first rays of the morning sun crept through the open tent flap. Tying a chiffon scarf over her hair, Jayne picked up her sunglasses and ventured outside.

The early-morning winter air was crisp and chilly. The lack of mud on the hard sun-baked ground revealed the absence of rain during the night.

Yesterday Tariq has said that the clouds could dissipate into the ether, and he had been right, overhead the sky was a clear blue and the air smelt of dry desert dust. She scanned her surroundings, searching for Tariq. He wasn't in the immediate surrounds of the encampment. She walked around the tent, to where he'd parked the vehicle. It was gone.

Her heart jolted. Then she saw it parked a short way out in the shimmer of the desert. Nearby Jayne made out the form of a man and above his head hovered a falcon.

Tariq.

And Noor.

The distance over the desert was deceptive. It took her fifteen minutes of brisk walking to reach them. By the time she got there, Noor had returned to her master and sat perched on his glove.

Tariq turned his head. "Good morning. Did you sleep well?" Aside from the polite inquiry, Jayne could read little in the high-boned face, his dark gaze narrowed against the brightening light, but she sensed that he had withdrawn.

Why?

What had changed since last night when they drank coffee with the Bedouin, when she'd felt at ease with him? There'd been no coolness between them in the tent afterwards, before she'd bathed. To the contrary, there had been a flare of heat that she'd quickly doused. So why the feeling that they were now separated by a continent as cold and as vast as the Antarctic?

"Yes, I slept fine." Hadn't he? She examined his face. There were dark shadows beneath his eyes. Maybe not. Perhaps it was worry about his father that had kept him awake?

"Have you heard from the palace?"

He got her meaning. "I spoke to my father, he is sounding better. The nurse says he seems to have rallied and made an unexpected recovery." His gaze remained shadowed. "Not that it will change the ultimate outcome. But he does seem more comfortable."

His father would still die. "And at least he will be there when you return."

"*Inshallah.*"

If it is Allah's will. She sighed and examined the falcon. "I don't remember Khan wearing that," Jayne observed, changing the subject to one less bleak.

"That's a transmitter." Tariq's expression was hard to read. "I used to hunt the purist way, with no modern gadgets. But

I don't want to lose Noor, so I decided to make use of the technology at my disposal."

"What happened to Khan?"

"I lost him." His voice cooled even more. "Not long after you left."

Jayne decided against asking how. But her heart ached at the distance that yawned between them. And for a moment she longed for a replay of that moment when they'd laughed together while they'd shared that awful bitter coffee last night.

"But you still keep falcons," she said.

"Yes. It's a part of who I am, who I will always be."

Jayne suspected the statement held a warning. When he'd first brought her to Zayed she'd found the notion of hunting with falcons barbaric, a far cry from the romantic vision she'd carried in her head of nomadic Bedouin mounted on an Arab stallion while a falcon plummeted out of the sky to ride on the falconer's arm.

"You're a sheikh. And a falconer." There was a finality in her words. He was a world apart from her. They had nothing in common.

"And a man."

She stiffened at the flat, emotionless statement. Yet it reminded her of exactly what they did have in common. *He was a man.* His hot golden eyes reminded her of the fact. An ache stirred deep within her as their gazes entwined. *She was a woman.* They were bound together by threads of desire.

By sex.

And nothing else.

She broke the connection and looked away, reluctant to consider the unruly attraction that had existed between them. That was in the past. But was it? The kiss he'd pressed on her lips the other night flitted through her mind. Jayne shifted uncomfortably as she recalled her ardent response. The attraction was far from over. Noor shifted restlessly on his arm, drawing her gaze. Sucking a deep breath into her starved lungs, she said desperately, "Tell me why you became a falconer."

"I was five years old when I went with my father into the desert and experienced my first falcon hunt." His voice was low. "The Emirs are descended from the Bedu, it is customary for the ruling Emir to teach his son the tenets of falconry. I had not yet started school. I will never forget it. It was a memorable time of my life—less than a month later my mother left us."

Jayne recoiled. "I didn't know you remembered your mother. But you would've seen her from time to time afterwards?" Tariq's blatant refusal to discuss his mother had roused her curiosity. She hadn't noticed it in the past. She'd been young…in love…wrapped up in Tariq and later in her own misery.

"Every autumn houbara bustards fly south from the northern hemisphere to Africa and stop off in Zayed," Tariq continued, ignoring her question. "Peregrine and saker falcons migrate a little earlier. The canny Bedu falconers saw a way to supplement a sparse diet of milk, dates and bread. They would have only a couple of weeks before the houbara arrived. So they would trap a falcon and have to train it in a few weeks. The bird became a coveted ally to hunt houbara, which are good eating—considered by the bedu to be a gift from God through the winter months."

Jayne stared out over the timeless stretch of the desert. It was bleak and forsaken. He wasn't going to talk about his mother. Not to her. But at least that awful taciturn silence had been broken. And she couldn't help wondering if his mother had felt as out of place in the desert as she Jayne. She shivered. Beside her, Noor cocked her head and spread her wings before lifting gracefully into the air. "Is she hungry?"

"Probably. Noor missed a flock of pigeons earlier—they'd had a head start. I called her back."

"Will she find prey?"

Tariq shrugged. "If she doesn't I have a lure with meat in the truck." He tipped his head to the SUV. "But after the time spent in the *kafas* yesterday I wanted to give her a chance to fly for at least an hour before I cage her for the rest of the drive. There's a lot of space in the desert for her to stretch her wings. And plenty of birds for her to prey on."

"Plenty of birds? Here?" Jayne gave the surrounding wasteland a pointed stare.

He moved closer. "Yes, there are—more than a decade ago when the falcon and houbara populations became seriously endangered, I had to implement breeding programs throughout Zayed for both the falcons and the houbara. Now captive birds are released annually."

"So that falconers can hunt?" she challenged, tilting her head back to stare into his face.

"Without the hunters, there would be no falcons and no houbara—except for a few wild birds in zoos and the last of the numbers of the extinct birds stuffed for display in museums." He loomed over her. "Is that what you want?"

"No," she admitted, her attention fixed on his exquisitely moulded mouth.

"And there would be less people learning the ways of the desert and passionate about conserving the habitat that these creatures live in."

Passionate. Her breath caught. Finally she murmured, "I suppose."

Words spilled from Tariq. "I fiercely believe the ancient tenets that have come from our forefathers. A falconer should have love and respect for both the falcon and the quarry and have a deep concern for the hunting territory and environment."

Love and respect. That's what she'd craved from him. But bringing her to Zayed had killed his love. And she'd learned he'd never had any respect for her…for her love. As if it were yesterday she could remember him storming into the library where she sat with Roger talking about books they'd both read while he mended a first-edition copy of *The Letters of Pliny to the Consul* with reverent fingers.

Tariq had taken one look at their heads bent over the ancient book and demanded that she come with him at once. He'd been so furious that his eyes had blazed with a tigerish light and the generous mouth she'd loved so much had been set in a thin, implacable line.

Even now the memory caused her stomach to cramp into a cold, tight ball.

Jayne breathed slowly. In. Out. In again. She fought to relax and tried to concentrate on what he was saying.

"My forefathers released their falcons into the wild at the end of the hunting season—but now with more wealth after the discovery of oil in Zayed, falconers are keeping the better birds. So I have put a program in place where at the end of each season some sakers and peregrine falcons bred in captivity, who are trained in September and hunt through the winter, are released."

The falcons were far luckier than she had been. He hadn't released her. He had banished her, despite her tears…her pleas. He had been ruthless.

"Each season I personally train one bird that I will release—to join the wild population and strengthen the blood-line. That bird will be equipped with a transmitter and tracked by satellite to add to research on bird migration."

"I must admit, I didn't think of the hunter as carer," Jayne said. "If I thought of it at all, I thought of the lone nomad on his horse with his falcon strapped to his wrist."

Tariq gave a short, unamused laugh. "That age is gone. The world has changed. Falconry has changed. In the past, falcon-ers followed on horseback or on camel—now we use four-wheel-drives. And GPSs and transmitters."

She gave him a once-over, taking in the *thobe* he wore, his dark tanned face. He looked like an ancient desert warrior. Timeless. Fierce. Unforgiving. Yet he was as com-fortable negotiating state affairs abroad in a western business suit as he was here in the desert. "Do you miss the old Zayed?"

"It doesn't matter whether I miss it. Everything changes. *Inshallah.*" Something about the finality in the way he said the last made her suspect that he was thinking about his father. Once he died, Tariq's whole world would change again. His father would be gone, he could become the Emir of Zayed, a man powerful beyond belief…and he would grant her the divorce she wanted.

Nothing stayed the same.

Not even the desert. The dunes shifted under the fingers of the wind just like the evil whispers of the Emir had forever changed Tariq's love for her to hate.

A lump rose in the back of her throat. "Where is Noor?" she asked a trifle huskily. "Hasn't she had enough time up there? I need some breakfast."

"We must wait. A popular saying in falconry is: 'Who is training whom?'" He flashed her a grim smile. "The falconer must learn great patience…and trust."

Her heart turned over.

He smiled far too little these days. Even that sorry attempt had to be worth something. And he'd never trusted much at all. "You mean that you trust that Noor will come back?"

"Yes." His certainty was unequivocal. "And if you're hungry, there are some cereal bars in the truck."

Jayne walked away to forage around and emerged with the foil-wrapped bars. She gave one to Tariq. He tore the wrapper off and his teeth tore into the bar.

Those same teeth had once closed gently on her flesh… teasing…evoking delight and pleasure.

Looking away up into the empty sky, Jayne asked huskily, "How do you know Noor is still here? That she hasn't flown away?"

"Watch this." Tariq aimed the antenna at the empty sky and the signal boomed. "See? She's there. Right above us. Watching every move we make."

"Amazing." Jayne squinted upward, the light so bright, that even with sunglasses she needed to screw up her eyes.

A few minutes later Tariq breathed out. "Ah, now things are about to get interesting."

Jayne took in the change in him. The cool remote air had gone. His admiration for the falcon shone from his eyes. He'd transformed into a man of action, in his element. A falconer.

"See that?" Tariq was pointing at a bird about the size of a heron, flying swiftly towards them. "That's a houbara bustard, Noor's favourite prey." He placed an arm around her shoulders. "Come."

Under the weight of his touch, Jayne froze, her breath catching in her throat.

Breathe.

In. Out. In again.

"What are you waiting for? Hurry."

His grip tightened and a wave of emotion shook her. She sought desperately for something to say. "But it's so big. I mean, that's not a pigeon or something."

Far above them something flashed. Noor.

Jayne started to move.

"She's hunting." Tariq opened the passenger door of the SUV for her and slammed it behind her. An instant later he slid in beside her. "Noor will need all her skill to track down a bird of that size and speed. A falcon needs to hit a houbara hard to take it out and knock it to the ground. Noor is less skilled on the ground than in the air, and faced with a larger prey on the desert floor she may suffer injury if it can still fight."

"I hope she doesn't get hurt." Concern for the graceful falcon swept through Jayne.

Tariq turned his head to look at her. His gaze skimmed her face. Jayne's breath caught at the sudden spark of warmth in his eyes. For an instant time slowed, then he blinked. And the moment was past.

"Noor is a survivor." The SUV surged forward. "Let's go find her."

Six

Two kilometres on, Tariq and Jayne were still chasing behind the bustard with Noor hunting a long way above.

"She'll be exhausted," Jayne said in disbelief.

"Noor can fly for about an hour making repeated strikes. At the moment she's taking advantage of stealth," Tariq explained. "See how she flies above the houbara, with the sun at her back?" Jayne nodded. "The houbara won't see her coming."

"Good grief."

Just then the falcon tucked her wings and went into a dive, closing in on the bustard. Tariq pulled to a stop, and they both leaped out the vehicle. Even from the ground Jayne could hear the wind whistling through the peregrine's wings.

Tariq moved, hooking his arm around her shoulders.

When Noor struck, Jayne looked away. Tariq pulled her

into the crook of his arm. Her face buried in the heavy cotton of his *thobe,* she breathed in the rich, masculine scent of him.

When she raised her face from his shoulder the houbara was on the ground and Noor stood over her prey, her head bowed, ready to feast.

"She's waiting for my signal." Tariq gave a short sharp whistle and the bird started to eat. His hand rubbed up and down Jayne's arm, steadying her, offering rough comfort.

But the shivers that followed in the wake of his touch, had little do with comfort. Jayne bit her lip, determined not to let the melting sensation that pooled in her stomach undermine her good sense.

"Noor will not eat the prey without my consent," Tariq explained, the light rubbing of his fingertips torturing her. "If I were a nomad falconer, the bustard would feed more than only the falcon, and Noor would fly to hunt again."

It was savage. Jayne stared blindly at the bird. The desert was unforgiving. And the man beside her holding her was every bit as ruthless…yet once she had loved him with all her young heart. And he'd loved her with tenderness and reverence. Before his father had interfered and driven them apart.

When the falcon had finished, she fluttered over to them, half hopping, half skipping. She gave a cackle, breaking the silence.

"You're pleased with yourself, aren't you?" The falcon tilted her head at the gentle note in Tariq's voice and allowed him to squirt water from a spray bottle over her head and back. Noor closed her eyes, and Jayne could see her enjoyment.

"She's hot and tired." Jayne wished that Tariq spoke to her in that proud, soothing voice.

"See how full her crop is? Now she's ready to go back to her perch."

"Like a well-trained, tame female," Jayne said with a bite.

He looked at her through slitted, unreadable eyes. "Noor may be trained…but she will never be tame. Nor would I want her to be."

Glancing away, Jayne found herself staring into the dark bottomless gaze of a wild falcon. In that instant she felt a bond with the peregrine and something moved deep within her chest. Jayne was shaken by a strange sense that she balanced on the cusp of a revelation.

About the nature of the desert.

About Tariq.

And about herself.

Jayne glanced at Tariq. Why had she never noticed the untamed quality that clung to him? How had she ever mistaken him for another ordinary student in London on a backpacking holiday? Even when she'd learned he was studying finance, working in a London bank, the warning signs still hadn't gone off. She'd—mistakenly—imagined he worked as a clerk. And when she'd finally found out that he was a sheikh, the son of the Emir of Zayed, why had she ever imagined that she could domesticate such a man?

He was still so wrong for her…for what she wanted out of life. A man who loved her, a family, an ordinary existence. Yet she couldn't break the disquieting sense that after today nothing would ever be the same.

An hour later they had said their farewells to Ghayth and Matra and the rest of the tribe and were back on the road to Aziz. Tariq was exquisitely aware of the subtle scent that pervaded the vehicle. It came from Jayne's hair, from the shampoo he'd handed her in the bath last night. The memory of the want…the need…that had ripped through him while he stood beside his bathing wife was unwelcome. As was the inexplicable affinity he'd felt with her while Noor hunted.

Jayne hated the desert…hated falcons…considered him barbaric. How could he have felt such an unspoken bond with her, in the place she hated most? And he couldn't afford to feel any sort of affinity or desire for her.

It was not acceptable.

He lapsed back into brooding silence.

He would've preferred the foreboding from yesterday, the threat of the thunderstorm, to the fragile tension that stretched across the wasteland between them.

"Where do those tracks lead?" Jayne's voice broke the rising tension.

Tariq followed her arm to where she pointed at a sandy desert byway—little more than goat track—that branched off from the main road. "Most lead to grazing camps. They're access roads so that provisions and fodder for livestock can be delivered."

"Livestock?" Jayne sounded disbelieving. "It's hard to believe that anything survives in this hostile terrain."

Resentment surged within him, rising to sit hot and tight in his throat. "It's only hostile to you because you hate it so much. Many consider the desert beautiful."

"Maybe hate is too strong a word." She hesitated. He had the feeling she was groping for words. "After I fell ill on our camel trip, I wasn't in a hurry to repeat the excursion. Perhaps I just don't understand this world."

"It's my world."

Jayne didn't respond. She simply turned her head and stared out the window. And that gave Tariq no satisfaction at all. It certainly did nothing to quell the heat in his groin.

Don't think about it…and it might subside.

Sure.

To get his attention off the predicament that filled his thoughts—and tightened his briefs beneath the *thobe*—he tried to imagine the desert through her eyes. Bleak. Endless. Foreign. This far north the desert was much more sandy—less stony—and there were tufts of greenery that stretched as far as the eye could see.

"The desert changes as we travel north," he said, relenting a little. It wasn't her fault he wanted her. By Zayed, she'd made it clear that she couldn't wait to be rid of him. She didn't want him; his wife already had a new man lined up.

Neil.

Blond. Pale eyes. A man who'd grown up a stone's throw from where she had, according to the investigator's report. Who'd attended the same schools and churches as she had. A man who shared her upbringing…her world…and was everything he wasn't.

"There's actually some greenery here. Kind of like seagrass on a beach," she agreed and pointed out the window.

Tariq suppressed his infuriating thoughts and bent his head to follow her arm. "Those scrubby bushes provide cover for the wintering populations of houbara. Desert warbler and wheatear also inhabit this area. In spring they will return to the central Asian steppes to breed."

"Oh."

"Not so inhospitable. The desert teems with life. There are lizards and beetles and at night the gerbils come out. This area is a conservation habitat. No hunting is allowed."

"Not even for Noor?"

"Not even with falcons. Beyond this conservation area lies

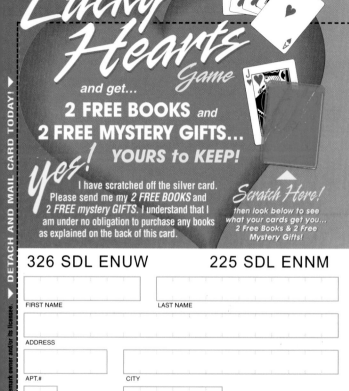

▼ DETACH AND MAIL CARD TODAY! ▼

Play the Lucky Hearts Game

and get...

2 FREE BOOKS and
2 FREE MYSTERY GIFTS...

YOURS to KEEP!

yes! I have scratched off the silver card.
Please send me my *2 FREE BOOKS* and
2 FREE mystery GIFTS. I understand that I
am under no obligation to purchase any books
as explained on the back of this card.

Scratch Here!
then look below to see
what your cards get you...
2 Free Books & 2 Free
Mystery Gifts!

326 SDL ENUW

225 SDL ENNM

FIRST NAME

LAST NAME

ADDRESS

APT.#

CITY

STATE/PROV.

ZIP/POSTAL CODE

(S-D-11/07)

Twenty-one gets you
2 FREE BOOKS and
2 FREE MYSTERY GIFTS!

Twenty gets you
2 FREE BOOKS!

Nineteen gets you
1 FREE BOOK!

TRY AGAIN!

The Silhouette Reader Service™ — Here's how it works:

the border with Bashir, and Sheikh Karim has declared an even larger corridor of desert a protected reserve, all the way down to the gulf. So when we get to Aziz, Noor will have to be fed from a lure, as hunting is completely banned."

"I want a falcon."

Tariq shot her a disbelieving glance. From her expression, the words had surprised Jayne as much as they had Tariq. His mouth twisted and he couldn't stop the cynicism that escaped. "Soon you'll be back in New Zealand…in the city. Where will you keep a falcon? Fly it?"

"I'll find somewhere. There must be clubs."

"And what will Neil say about your new…passion?" He drew out the "sh" sound in the final word to a sibilant hiss and she recoiled, pressing against the door. But she didn't reply. Fixing his attention back on the road, he gave a harsh bark of laughter. But he found no humour in the situation. Finally he said, "You've never appreciated anything from Zayed, why would you want a falcon?"

"What do you want me to say? Because I might grow to understand the power and secret of the desert?" Even as his head snapped around to stare at her, she was saying dismissively, "No, nothing as deep as that. Noor is so graceful. And I'd like the challenge of training a falcon like her."

For a moment, there, she'd had him going. But she'd been mocking him. If he'd thought that she would want to learn the ways of Zayed…he shook away the thought. *No.* It would make absolutely no difference. He didn't want her back, dared not take her back. "You'll need a lot of patience. Some birds are far more headstrong than Noor."

"I have a lot of patience."

He looked across at her. "So much patience that only a few

months after our marriage you fell into bed with another man and betrayed me?"

Jayne went very still. A sideways glance revealed her hands fisted in her lap, the knuckles white. Then she turned her head, and he caught a glimpse of eyes stretched wide with shock before he returned his attention to the road.

There'd been more than shock in her eyes. There'd been bewilderment…a gut-wrenching devastation that he'd torn open the subject that was tacitly understood to be taboo.

But this time she didn't shrink away. "Doesn't it strike you as strange that I demanded a marriage contract where you could have only one wife, and then I committed adultery?"

She hurled the words at him. For a very brief timespan he felt confusion, then he shrugged. "Since when has a marriage contract been a guarantee that one of the parties will not stray? That clause only meant you didn't want to risk your position. There was no guarantee if I married again, you'd be senior wife."

"You don't think that maybe I wanted our marriage to be a monogamous, once-in-a-lifetime love?"

"If that were the case, you wouldn't now want a divorce." Unable to look at her, he glared at the road ahead. "If that were the case, there would be no Neil waiting back for you in Auckland."

"Oh, what the hell is the point? First it was poor Roger and now it's Neil. You're never going to trust me. And I no longer want to be married to someone who doesn't trust me. It's as simple as that."

"Do not speak his name." He swerved off the road, yanked up the hand brake and swung to glare at her, baring all the rage and anguish he'd suppressed for years. "It's not simple at all. Not only did you betray me, you fell pregnant with the infidel's child."

She gave a gasp. The long, level look she gave him was filled with hurt and sorrow. The reproach kicked at his gut like a mule. But he refused to be swayed, to soften. "Less than fifty years ago, you would've been stoned to death in my country for such a blatant betrayal of your husband, do you know that?"

She stared back at him, her face cold and set like marble.

"Do you know that?" He wanted to shake her. Instead he clenched his hands around the steering wheel, terrified he might put his hands around her throat and choke her. "Have you any idea of what you did?" Her betrayal had emasculated him.

"Instead of a stoning, you accused me and banished me. You wouldn't listen—"

"To what? There was enough evidence. And you refused to take a DNA test—"

"An insult!"

"If you were innocent, you would never have hesitated to take the DNA test."

Jayne gave a groan of frustration. "Do you think I wanted a husband who needed a DNA test to prove that the child I carried was his?" Her face was tight and pale. "I wanted you to listen to my side—"

"I was so enthralled by you, I wasn't letting you whisper seductive, traitorous lies to me."

"Is that what your father said? That I would sway you with sex and lies?" Her velvet brown eyes were colder and harder than he'd ever seen them. "That's why you wouldn't listen to me? Because of your father's warped opinions?"

"That's what you always do. Bring my father into to it. You know that's a sure way to rile me."

"Didn't I have the right to defend myself?" Her voice rose. Then she went silent. Finally she said, "We can't have this discussion…or any discussion about the breakdown of our marriage…without bringing your father into it."

"I don't want to hear your poisonous lack of respect for my father. You sinned. You committed *zina*. I should've thrown you into prison. Instead I let you off lightly, I told you never to set foot in Zayed again."

He'd been enraged. And she'd left. He'd found her passport on their marital bed together with her wedding ring and known she would never return. The plain gold band she'd insisted on choosing, little knowing that the man who she was marrying could buy her anything in the exclusive jeweller's shop. That had been one of the things he'd loved about her.

The grief that had stormed through him after her departure had been fierce. He'd loved her with his whole heart. Then hated her with his entire existence. All that was left was to forget her, to drown himself in the Zayedi affairs of state… travelling abroad…keeping busy from daybreak to long after sundown. Until even his father had looked troubled.

In the years since, he'd tried never to speak of his wife. Unless pressed. Then she'd called demanding a divorce, and suddenly her name was everywhere.

"It's fortunate that you miscarried the child." He remembered the brief, bleak little letter she had sent him, several months after she had left:

I lost the baby.
Jayne

A couple of stark typed lines on a white sheet of paper. He'd torn it from side to side and hurled it in the bin. He'd been glad in a bitter kind of way. With the loss of the baby, the life she and the infidel had created had been lost forever. He remembered the humiliating moment of hesitation…the damning instant when he'd considered finding her, bringing her back to Zayed. He'd prayed for his soul that night.

And he'd resisted, humiliated by her evil act, which he knew would lead the way to others in the future. The shame of desiring a woman who took other lovers while married to him had been too much.

"Fortunate?" It was a low grunt of pain.

"The child might have grown up blond like his infidel father announcing your adultery to the world." Tariq didn't know what devil rode him.

"I don't want to talk about this." Her voice was ragged, and her dark lashes fell against her bleached cheeks.

After a long moment of silence, Tariq said, "Have it your way." Viciously he swung the vehicle back onto the road and stepped on the gas.

But last night, in that Bedu tent, Tariq knew he had come face-to-face with his demons. In spite of her ignominious betrayal, he still desired his wife. And he feared he would never be free of the silken threads of wanting her.

Not even after the divorce.

"What is that?"

As the angle of the hill slowed the SUV, Jayne roused herself from the silence she'd buried herself in for the last section of the drive and stared up at the dark stone building that rose in front of them.

"Mahood's, er, château."

"His what?"

"It's an old fort. Very historical," Tariq replied grimly, accelerating a little up the hill to the fort.

"It looks like the prison you said I was lucky to avoid." Jayne drew a deep, shuddering breath. Could it get any worse? She could've kicked herself as tension filled the car. "Like the kind of place that has dungeons and racks and implements specially designed for torture. Or, if I wanted to be fanciful, I could say it reminded me of Dracula's castle." She caught her bottom lip between her teeth. "If I go in, will I ever come out?" She was only half-joking.

"Don't worry. The walls are there to keep the inhabitants safe."

Jayne wasn't so sure about that.

"Relax, I guarantee that you'll be safe."

She gave a snort. "Thanks, your guarantees truly reassure me."

"Sarcasm doesn't become you, wife," he growled. "Now let us go and greet our hosts."

Another even less pleasant surprise awaited Jayne inside the fort. Leila—the woman the Emir had been desperate for Tariq to marry all those years ago, stood beside Ali, her father. Jayne shuddered inside. Could it get any worse? She should have expected with his wife dead, that Ali would need a hostess.

Leila inspected Jayne from head to toe through dark sullen eyes. When she'd finished, a dismissive smile twisted her henna-painted lips. Tariq moved closer to Jayne and put an arm around her shoulder. Jayne stiffened in surprise.

"Would you show us to our room? My wife is tired."

Leila's head jerked back at the reproof. "This way."

For the first time in several hours, Jayne started to feel a little more cheerful. Tariq kept his arm around her waist, and she was grateful for the support he offered.

Leila led them down a long gloomy corridor. Several twists and turns later, Jayne decided the fort could well be a place of torture. A short flight of stairs took them past a landing where slits in the walls for archers indicated the building's past purpose.

"Here, this is your room." Leila opened the door and they stepped into a large chamber with an immense canopied bed. On the far side of the room, latticed shutters had been flung open to reveal a view over the desert. But Jayne couldn't get her eyes off that bed.

One bed.

How had she thought things had gotten as bad as they could?

Clearly she and Tariq were expected to share that sensually draped bed. Images jumbled through her head like a relentless slide show. Tariq touching her, making love to her. Tariq telling her to go and never come back. Tariq kissing her the other night in his study. Her inability to resist. Tariq's hurtful conviction that she'd betrayed him with another man.

The dent on the divan where another body had lain beside her last night…

Jayne swung around. "I'm not staying here." Before she had finished speaking, she was heading for the door.

Leila's gaze glittered. "Our humble abode does not please the sheikhah?"

Tariq stepped forward. "Jayne—"

But his wife clearly wasn't in the frame of mind to be placated. "There's nothing wrong with the abode," Jayne said, her eyes flashing fire, her colour high. "But I have a problem with the accommodation."

"Exactly what is the sheikhah's problem?"

"Leila—" Tariq tried to intervene.

"I am not sleeping in that." Jayne pointed emphatically to the massive bed. "I want my own room."

Leila's gaze flickered between them, alight with avid curiosity.

Tariq felt fury and the familiar humiliation rush through his bloodstream. Before long everyone in Aziz would know that his errant wife refused to sleep with him. Leila would take great pleasure in spreading the gossip. By tomorrow it would reach Jazirah. He shut his eyes.

But would Leila guess what his wife really wanted? A divorce…

That rumour better not reach his father's ears. Not after he'd worked so hard to reassure the man he revered.

Leila stood in the doorway and smirked. "Of course, I will find the sheikhah a room of her own."

Jayne smiled sweetly at the other woman. "That would be lovely."

Leila had never been eager to lift a finger to assist Jayne. His wife had certainly never smiled at Leila with such glowing enthusiasm. Tariq decided he was ready to throttle them both.

Seven

That evening, accompanied by an elderly chaperone who had come to fetch her, Jayne left the pokey little room where Leila had installed her, daring her to object, and made her way to the reception rooms.

She stalked in, her head held high, ready to take on whoever gave her trouble.

Leila.

Ali.

Tariq.

She didn't care.

No one was getting the better of her tonight. For too long she'd allowed Tariq…his father…his political allies to walk all over her. No more.

But the sight of a young woman staring with dewy, adoring eyes up at Tariq was enough to stop Jayne in her tracks.

The nymph—she was barely old enough to be called a woman—wasn't touching Tariq…or even sharing extended eye contact, which could be dangerous, but she fluttered her lashes and every line of her body revealed her yearning. Suddenly Jayne felt quite ill.

She was thrust into the unwelcome mists of the past…of watching Leila making a play for Tariq. Of the poison the Emir had dripped into her ear about how Tariq should've married Leila. Not her. About the arrangement that had existed between Ali and the Emir that one day their children would marry and consolidate the northern and southern regions of the sheikhdom.

She swallowed. This young girl didn't carry the Emir's approval.

But she loved Tariq.

It was as clear as day to Jayne. Because once she, too, had yearned for him. Once upon a time *she* had gazed at him with soft velvety eyes, full of trust and love.

She looked away, not wanting to intrude on the girl's naked infatuation. And caught sight of Leila staring at the pair with unveiled hatred in her eyes.

Jayne's stomach cramped. The hairs on the back of her neck prickled. There was trouble coming. She could smell it.

To avoid the nastiness, she made her way to a table laden with *mezze* at the back of the room and helped herself to *kibbe,* the small, tasty, round balls of minced meat.

"You must be English."

She looked up at the man who had spoken in a transatlantic drawl. "No, I'm from New Zealand. Where are you from?"

"Texas," he said with a grin that deepened the laugh lines around hazel eyes. "Oil country."

Her spirits lifted at the wide uncomplicated pleasure in his face and she smiled back. "I should've known."

"Dexter." He stuck out a hand.

She took it and followed his lead, relieved that the anonymity of first names did away with the need for explanation. "Jayne."

"Now that you know what I do, it's your turn to tell me."

"I'm a teacher. But in the last couple of years I've become increasingly interested in literacy—so I'm studying further."

"So that's why you're here. To do research?"

She didn't correct him. Didn't want the questioning stares, the pointed silence when he discovered she was the sheikh's estranged wife.

Instead she started to talk about what she'd seen so far, about the education levels in Zayed and the Bedouin women in the desert, and he nodded, looking far more fascinated than the subject warranted. To head him off from getting any ideas about furthering their acquaintance, she said, "I must go find my husband."

"You're married?"

Not for much longer. But for once the thought no longer brought the delight it had only days ago. Unsmilingly, she nodded.

"He's a fool to leave you unattended."

What could she say to that? He always had. Tariq was too important to spend time chasing after her. "I had better go."

Tariq glanced around impatiently. Where was Jayne? He hadn't seen his wife since she'd stormed out of his bedchamber earlier. And he'd been too furious to find her later.

At his side stood Karim's stepmother, and her daughter, Yasmin. Yasmin asked him something, her voice soft and breathy. Irritatingly so, because he had to lean forward to make out what she was saying. From across the room he could feel the weight of Karim's gaze. Had Karim already heard the gossip? That Jayne had fled her husband's bed-chamber?

He frowned. Where the hell was Jayne? What was taking her so long? He needed her. He certainly didn't need Karim gaining the wrong impression about his intentions to Yasmin. Especially not after he'd taken such pains to twart his father's matchmaking attempts.

Just then he caught sight of the older woman who had been sent to collect Jayne from her room and escort her down. He touched her arm, lightly, getting her attention. "Was the sheikhah not ready to come down?"

The woman gave him a puzzled stare. "The sheikhah is here."

Here? *Where?* Tariq's head whipped around.

He barely heard Yasmin droning on about her favourite horse. Instead he froze as he caught sight of his wife.

She was laughing.

Yes, laughing—when she barely smiled with him—up at a strange man. A westerner with blondish hair and tanned features. Just like—

Tariq raked a hand through his hair. No, he was not think-ing about that. Not now. So he looked down at Yasmin. Her eyes were dark and glowing. Biddable. Waiting for him to say yes to whatever it was that she had asked.

Tariq muttered a reply, barely conscious of the words he was stringing together. Then, unable to help himself, he searched for Jayne again. She was still with the American who worked for Ali. Unable to bear looking at them any longer, he glanced away and caught a glimpse of Leila, hidden in a group of women. She was staring straight at him. Although he couldn't decipher her expression, a shadow passed over him. Jayne had always referred to the sensation as a goose walking over a grave. He'd hated the expression.

But it captured the malevolence Leila radiated.

How could this be? Why was it that the only woman he wanted was the woman he had driven away? The woman talking to another man...the woman who wanted nothing from him—except a divorce. And why could he not get her out of his mind? The memory of her dewy skin in the bath, the sweet taste of her mouth beneath his.

He was weak. He couldn't resist the sensual memories. And he'd thought he'd been so smart. When Jayne had contacted him about a divorce, he'd seen a way to let his father die in peace, satisfied his son was happily married. The last thing he had expected when his wife returned was to discover that he still desired his wife.

A wife who he could not keep faithful...a wife who hated Zayed.

What the hell was he to do?

Yasmin was speaking again, about the Arabian stud in Bashir where some of the world's finest horses had been bred. He listened with one ear, but his attention kept straying to Jayne, resenting the easy way she was talking to the geologist, her hands waving as she expressed herself. She looked relaxed and at ease, a far cry from the wary, tense woman who had pressed herself up against the door and watched him with cautious eyes when he'd pulled over at the side of the road only a few hours ago.

Why couldn't she relax like that with him? He gazed at her with a growing hunger. Why was she strung so tight when they were alone together? Was it their cultures that separated them, that made her unable to relax? Or was it him?

The thought made his heart burn with pain.

He wanted her to smile at him. He wanted her to talk to him with the same eagerness she spoke to the complete stranger in front of her.

So he glared across the room at her.

"The sheikhah's preferences for blond westerners are well-known." The soft murmur came from Yasmin. "It looks like this man fits her requirements."

Rage exploded within Tariq. He turned on the young woman. "You should not listen to scandalous gossip. You know nothing about what man fits my wife's requirements. If you did you'd know I was that man."

"But she refuses you, a sheikh!"

So even Yasmin had heard that Jayne wouldn't share his bedchamber and was willing to take advantage of the opportunity to gain his attention. No doubt Yasmin knew that he had banished his wife because she had bedded another man. Humiliation scorched him.

"And you will be Emir when—" She must have read something in his face because she broke off, her hand covering her mouth.

"When my father dies."

"I am sorry, I was impertinent."

Tariq bowed his head. "No. It is I who must apologise."

Yasmin might be young but she wasn't stupid. She instantly understood why he was apologising. And her eyes filled with tears. "So you will not marry me? Not ever?" Yasmin's lower lip trembled. "But Karim says—"

"I know what your brother thinks. He's been trying to

broker a marriage between you and me for months. It is not going to happen. And the Emir should have conveyed that. There will be someone else for you. One day."

More tears welled in the eyes in front of him. "It will be too late."

Tariq cursed in English. At the shock in her eyes, he apologised. "You were not meant to understand that."

A silver tear spilled onto her cheek. "Is it me? Is there something wrong with me? Am I not a good enough woman for you?"

Frustration surged inside him. And fury at Jayne. His wife should have been beside him to prevent this, not standing talking—no, laughing—with another damned man. "There is nothing wrong with you. It is with me—I am not a good enough man."

"You, come with me!"

Jayne stiffened at the high-handed command. It reminded her of that day in the palace library with Roger when Tariq had swept in and uttered the same words. All hell had broken loose afterward. She was not in the mood for a repeat performance. She was tempted to refuse. Then she shrugged. What could he do?

"How dare you shame me, make me the laughingstock of Zayed!"

Tariq's hand was hard under her elbow. Unused to the length of the kaftan swirling around her legs, she had to take small running steps to keep up with him.

"I will not share a bedchamber with you."

In a quiet corner of the room, he stopped and swung her round to face him. He moved closer. "Did I do anything to you last night? Did I touch you? Seduce you?"

Mutely she shook her head. Had she imagined that simmering tension between them earlier in the desert this morning? Or had the flare of desire all been one-sided? On her side only? Colour flooded her. She felt the blush rising up her throat, over her cheeks. She'd made a complete fool of herself. Clearly Tariq had no desire to touch her….

"What on earth possessed you to say such a thing to Leila of all people?"

"What do you mean 'Leila of all people'? You almost married the woman."

"Never." His eyes bored into hers. "I would never have married her."

"She still wants you. *Her* father thinks she would have made you a better wife. And *your* father wanted you to marry her."

"Please, let's not go down that road again. You're prejudiced against my father and I've grown weary of it." With his free hand Tariq brushed his hair back. "Leila is married to another, it's all academic now."

Jayne swung on her heel. "And I'm weary of all this." She swept a hand around indicating the throng. "I'm going to my room."

He jerked her back. "Oh, no, you're not."

"Where are you taking me?"

"I want you to stay beside me," he spoke through tight lips. "Where I can see you."

Jayne's spine grew ramrod straight. So this was about her conversation with the tall Texan.

"Why? So that no one else can talk to me?" Nothing had changed. Tariq still suspected her every move. Boy, she would be pleased to get out of here.

"I brought you with me to keep Yasmin at bay. I don't need trouble with Karim."

Yasmin?

The young besotted-looking woman.

And then the penny dropped….

"You brought me all this way as protection, didn't you?" He didn't answer. But he didn't need to. The flush of blood high on his cheekbones told all. "Body armour for you to wear to ward off other women." She turned away, infuriated.

"See it from my perspective. I don't want to alienate Karim. And he's been angling—".

"For you, the oh-so-desirable sheikh, the future Emir of Zayed, to marry his half sister—and create a dynasty linking two countries." To think she'd pitied Yasmin. Such a political match would undoubtedly have the Emir's approval. "Except there's one problem from Yasmin's point of view— you're still married to me."

"Soon you will leave Zayed, you will get the divorce you want so badly and once you're gone I have no intention of putting my head back into the bridal noose."

"What about your father's wishes for you to settle?"

Something shifted in his eyes. Then he shrugged. "My father will be dead. He won't know. And if he can see me from the paradise of the afterlife then it won't be the first time I have disappointed him."

He was referring to their misguided marriage.

Jayne couldn't resist the wicked self-flagellistic impulse to say, "You could do worse than Yasmin, you know. She's in love with you."

Tariq's jaw hardened. "She only thinks she is—mostly because her brother encouraged the fantasy."

"Without any help from you?" She raised an eyebrow. "How did he get that idea?"

"A long story." He sighed and rubbed a hand over his face. The lines were deeply etched. He looked tired and dispirited. Instantly her heart softened.

"So what have you told her?"

"Nothing. But Karim knows I am married to you and I'm not allowed another wife in terms of our marriage agreement." There was a bitter edge to his voice. Jayne wasn't sure she wanted to know more.

"I'm glad you remember that." But the topic had set her thoughts straying down a forbidden path. Her husband was a very virile man. They had been apart for years. "Not that a little thing like a marriage contract would stop you taking what you want."

He stiffened. The gold eyes were alight with anger. "What are you implying? I am a man of honour. Unlike my wife, I do not commit *zina*—no adultery, no extramarital sex."

Eight

Jayne had a sudden urge to smack Tariq.

He sounded so damned pious. She could imagine the uproar that such an act would cause, if the recalcitrant wife struck the sheikh. It was almost worth doing, simply to measure the reaction. She subdued the mad urge. "So, will you marry her after we divorce?" A funny little pain lodged under her heart. She didn't want to think of Tariq married to another woman. Not even the young and nubile Yasmin.

It shocked her.

Since when was her mission to gain a divorce no longer the most pressing desire in the world? Why did she suddenly want to spend time with Tariq...to delay the day of departure? She *must* be mad.

"No." He shook his head. "She's too young."

"She's utterly beautiful," Jayne said wistfully. "Those dark liquid eyes, her cheekbones, that slender figure."

"Beauty is nothing," he said disparagingly. "Dress up a stick and you get a doll."

"Easy for you to say," she muttered. He didn't know what it was like to be plain, never to attract a second look. Except from him. "Why did you ask me to have coffee with you that day in the Tate Gallery?"

"You had a beautiful smile."

"So you married me because you liked my smile?" she said facetiously. She'd been too bowled over by him, by the hot hunger in his eyes. Too busy falling in love with a man who was way out of her reach. If only she'd known who he really was.

"Not only your smile." This time there was a flash of that old hunger. "But you were gentle, too. Easygoing. And for the first time in my life I was with someone who made no demands of me. You've changed…you're not so—"

"Malleable?" She pursed her lips. "I was a doormat before." At least he didn't lie that it was her beauty that had blown him away. It was her lack of backbone more than her lack of beauty that he'd been drawn to, her very ordinariness. "Yasmin is young enough to be moulded. You could marry her and take another less beautiful wife, too. If that's what you want."

"One woman at a time is enough for me." Tariq's mouth twisted into a wry curve. "I think I want a woman who can stand up to me. A woman who has soft skin and silken hair… who responds like fire to my touch."

Jayne's breath caught. There was something in his voice… something that made her belly tighten and her breathing quicken.

Something primal.

Intimate.

Madness.

She stared at him her heart locked tight in her throat.

His chest lifted and fell. The silence stretched between them like a thread pulled tight. And then the silence snapped.

"Tariq."

Yasmin stood beside him. For an instant resentment surged through Jayne. *Why now?* Could the damn woman not have stayed away another moment or two?

Yasmin was making sheep eyes at him again. No, that was wrong. The young woman was too beautiful to be associated with a sheep. Her eyes were as wide and soft as a gazelle's, her mouth soft and trembling.

Jayne wanted to scream at Yasmin not to look at her husband like that. It was akin to an act of *zina*. The pang of poisonous emotion that pierced Jayne shocked her.

Jealousy. No! She couldn't feel possessive of Tariq. He was not hers. Could never be hers. Their worlds were simply too far apart.

And she had walked out of his world years ago.

Then the weight of his hand pressed against her side, propelling her forward. "Yasmin, I don't think you have met my wife, Jayne. You would've been a child when she first came to Zayed."

Hurt sparkled in the young woman's eyes at his implication that she was too young for him. The glint of silver tears, then she blinked. "No…I haven't." Her chin went up. "I thought you had left him years ago."

A declaration of war.

The unuttered "What are you doing back?" hung in the air.

How on earth was she to respond? Jayne glanced helplessly up at Tariq beseeching him for assistance.

He pulled her closer. Through her kaftan she could feel the

warmth of his body. "She's back now." Then one finger lifted her chin and he stared down into her eyes with a heat that melted the ruthless features. "Aren't you, *nuur il-en?*"

Jayne's heart skipped a beat as a pang of emotion stabbed her.

Steady on. This pretence was all for the benefit of the young woman watching. Tariq was simply using her to let Yasmin down. Gently.

So she nodded. And tried to smile, like a good, obedient wife would. Instead her gaze locked with his. At once the surroundings melted away. No one else existed. Except for her and Tariq. She thought she heard a stifled sob. And then Yasmin said, "You should never have left him. We all thought—"

"That the sheikh was a free man." Karim's voice broke in. "I would've welcomed him into the family—we grew up together."

Jayne wished Karim would shut up. Could he not see what he was doing to his sister? That he was making it so much worse?

"Even Leila has been praying for her husband to die of a heart attack, leave her a wealthy widow. There have been whispers of assassination. Leila would love to be Zayed's sheikhah."

"Stop." No hint of amusement lightened Tariq's expression. "You go too far, friend."

"Then I apologise." Karim bowed his head. "I apologise, too, for the trouble with Ali…and Mahood. It will not happen again."

"Hush, here comes Leila."

Through the black humour of the situation, Jayne felt a flash of pity for Tariq. The hunter had become the hunted…infinitely desirable prey to the women who fluttered around him.

What must it be like to be so in demand? To be so gorgeous, so powerful and wealthy that every woman in Zayed… and a few beyond its borders…wanted to ensnare him?

She stifled a laugh. But it really wasn't funny. All her life she'd wanted a man who was ordinary. Who worked a nine-to-five job at a bank and came home each night and helped her raise two children. A man like Neil. Instead she'd fallen for Tariq.

Gorgeous as sin.

A rich, powerful sheikh…who had turned her whole world upside down and brought her nothing but misery.

Yasmin and Leila and all the other beautiful vultures who fluttered around were welcome to him. He'd cost her too much. She'd already lost her heart…her baby…and her sanity.

Then his hand stroked up…over her hip, and heat shafted through her. For all her defiance she still wanted the damn man.

And the wanting did not ease the following day. Tariq had arranged to take Jayne on a tour of Aziz in the morning. He hoped to have the discussions with Mahood, Ali and Karim wrapped up the following morning and their departure the next day was already planned. While she appreciated his thoughtfulness, she could have done without the proximity to the one man in the world from whom she most wanted to escape.

The morning air was cool from the desert night. A blanket of wispy cloud was forming in the north, blocking out the pale-yellow sunlight.

Jayne wanted to see the *souqs,* the colourful exotic markets packed with everything to be found in Zayed. The outdoor camel *souq* smelt of the warm earthy creatures, and traders haggled in loud, booming voices. Jayne touched the soft nose of a gentle camel who poked her head out to be stroked. The animal's long feminine eyelashes reminded her of Yasmin.

"Come, let us move on," Tariq said, with a quick glance at the sky. Jayne looked, too. While she'd been absorbed with the camels, the clouds had closed in overhead, giving the day a dark, brooding closeness.

At the indoor carpet *souq,* Jayne admired a glorious array of rugs. Then they visited *souqs* for fresh products…bric-a-brac…copper and rugs.

And gold.

Jayne's eyes widened. Here at the gold *souq,* the loud market cacophony was absent. It was subdued, refined, clearly a place where large amounts of money changed hands. There were necklaces, intricately worked and set with stones in all colours. Fine gold chains with bells. The merchant inside straightened and preened at the sight of Tariq.

"Gold for the sheikhah, Excellency?"

"What would you like?" Tariq's face was expressionless. "You can have anything your heart desires. They even have ingots if you'd like one of those."

Her insides twisted into a heavy ball. Tariq thought the price of her heart's desire could be bought with an ingot of gold?

If only…

"You're joking?"

"Not at all." He indicated a safe in the wall. "In there. But I'm certain you'd prefer something a little prettier than a gold bar. Come." He walked toward her, his arm outstretched. "Have a look."

She folded her arms across her breasts and shrank away from him. "I don't want you to buy me gold."

His vivid eyes flared more brightly than any precious metal. And then emptied of all emotion as his arm dropped to his side. He turned to the merchant and started to talk rapidly in Arabic. Neither man paid her the least bit of attention as the merchant silently took trays out and offered them for Tariq's inspection.

Unable to help herself, Jayne peered into the trays. Pieces lay against dark velvet set with pearls and coral and turquoise. Necklaces. Rings. Bracelets. "They're beautiful."

"Turquoise is believed to ward off the evil eye," Tariq said.

Jayne bit her lip and refrained from asking whether it would protect her from his father. The Emir had caused her so much unhappiness. "These are pretty." She pointed to an ankle chain with gold bells.

"The noise from the bells will chase away evil spirits." Tariq nodded his head at the merchant who removed them from the tray.

"I don't want anything."

A young woman appeared from behind the heavy drape at the back of the *souq,* hips swaying from side to side.

"My daughter," the merchant pronounced with paternal pride.

She sashayed past Jayne with barely a glance before halting beside her father. She gave a little bob in Tariq's direction, her eyes veiled.

Jayne suppressed the urge to roll her eyes. But she shrank a little inside and retreated to the doorway, determined not to watch yet another women making a play for Tariq.

Through the entrance she could see the storm clouds rolling across the sky. No trace of sunlight remained. She could hear the low hum of Tariq's voice behind her, and a quick glance showed him handing payment to the young woman.

Leaning toward him, she handed Tariq a heavily embroidered satin bag.

Jayne cast the bag a disparaging look. Too small to hold an ingot, no doubt it held the gold she'd told Tariq she didn't want.

Now the woman was smiling, almost brushing up against Tariq. Indecent. If she leaned forward any further her *hijab* would fall off, Jayne thought acidly. Tariq thanked her. Disgusted with the byplay, Jayne turned to the door.

As they walked out to the waiting limousine, a gust of wind hit her like a blast.

"Steady." Tariq grabbed her elbow. Her mouth pursed, Jayne wrenched herself free. "Why are you sulking? Do you think that I'm going to seek that woman out and commit adultery? Is that what you believe me capable of? Yes, she made it clear that she was available."

"So why don't you marry her then?" Jayne burst out.

"She's not suitable. And she's probably already married. And in my experience it is the woman who starts down the road to adultery, not the man."

Jayne clambered into the backseat. Wherever they went there would always be fawning women. And given his mother's betrayal—the betrayal he would not even discuss—and her subsequent desertion of both Tariq and his father, it wasn't surprising he had so little respect for women. But she'd had enough.

Once seated, she said tightly, "You might want to consider what it has always been like for me. Wherever we go, women give me one disbelieving look, then they dismiss me and fall all over you."

"I've never encouraged them." He looked defensive. "So don't accuse—"

"I'm not accusing you of anything." The irony did not escape her. Of the two of them, she had far more grounds for suspicion. It would've been easy for Tariq to be unfaithful.

The limousine rolled forward. "It's my wealth."

Jayne stared at him and shook her head slowly. "It's much more than your wealth…or even your good looks."

He coloured, bright flags high on his slanting cheekbones, but held her gaze. "Oh, please."

"You're gorgeous, Tariq. And I'm plain old Jayne. I never thought I'd hold you—"

"That's why you put that clause in our marriage contract. You thought I would find another woman—betray you—make you the second wife!"

Now, with his acute gaze narrowed on her, she wished she hadn't started this, that she'd simply withdrawn into the background and let it pass. Why had she felt the need to reveal her annoyance? It simply hurt too much.

It was too late.

Finally she said with a sigh, "Maybe."

"So you didn't trust me—"

"I didn't trust my own appeal. I would've been a fool not to have insisted on that clause. What I'm trying to say is that you have charisma. You draw people—especially women—like bees to a honeypot. Even if you had not a cent to your name, no sheikhdom to rule, you'd still be inundated with women. And every waking hour I had to live with the fact that you were surrounded by adoring women who came on to you, regardless of my presence."

"I never wanted them."

Her breath caught at the ring of truth in his voice.

"All I ever wanted was you."

That had never been enough. "But your father didn't. I was never going to be good enough."

"My father wanted me to marry a woman of equal status—like he did. My mother was the youngest daughter of Socrates Kyriakos, the Greek shipping tycoon, she came with a dowry of millions and valuable access to supertankers. Their marriage was dynastic. It was about oil and its distribution all over the world. The Emir of Zayed marries for power and the consolidation of wealth. For strategic reasons." He must have seen the horror in her eyes because his voice gentled. "Jayne, you must understand, it's the way things have always been done in Zayed."

"So why did you marry me?"

He looked away. "I was young. Idealistic. A student living in London. I didn't want to follow the soulless example of my parents' marriage. My mother never loved my father—and she hated Zayed. She went on a holiday to see her family, fell pregnant. When my father found out, he told her to go."

"Didn't he give her a chance to defend herself? To tell him that the baby was his?"

"It wasn't his."

"How can you know that?"

"I overheard their fight. She told my father that she hated him, that she had someone else, someone who made her happy. She told him that she wanted to have her lover's child. She wanted a life. And that their marriage had been a mistake from the start—because they had married for oil and money." He looked up at her. His eyes held a vulnerability she'd never seen. "I didn't want that. By marrying you I broke the rules."

She shook her head. "So the Emir drove me away because my family was not rich and powerful enough. Even though I loved you more than anything in the world."

The softness…vulnerability…whatever it had been, vanished. "*I* drove you away. Not my father."

"Because of what you'd overheard two adults yelling at each other as a small child?"

"No!" It was a harsh, grating sound. "I drove you away for good reason, because you were unfaithful to me."

Jayne rolled her eyes skyward. "So we're back where we started, you still believe I betrayed you. In that case, there is nothing more to say."

"Wait." He caught her hand. "We're not back where we started. I never realised how insecure you were, after we came to Zayed, how little you trusted my love for you. It must have been terrible for you when I travelled abroad without you."

"Yes," she whispered. She looked down at her hands, not wanting him to see the misery in her eyes. She'd hated it when he'd gone north or gone abroad. A finger under her chin raised her face to his narrow-eyed inspection.

"You thought I was unfaithful." He paused. "Is that why you did it?"

The car had come to a standstill. They were back at the fort. With a last look at Tariq, Jayne reached for the door handle. As the door clicked open, she shook her head sadly. "I am not going to deny it again. I'm through with that. You must believe of me what you want."

"I am trying to understand," he said. "Help me."

"I can't," she said quietly. "This is something you're going to have to figure out for yourself."

Nine

Without waiting for the doorman, Jayne pushed open the door of the limousine and jumped out. The first heavy splats of rain hit her as she crossed the forecourt. Clutching her purse, she ran for cover. But the heavens opened and the rain came down in torrents.

In seconds she was drenched.

She reached the overhang of the portico at the front of the porch, out of breath and very, very wet. She leaped up a step, out of the path of the water that was already streaming around the base of the solid stone walls.

"Are you okay?" Tariq stood beside her. His white shirt clung to his torso, plastered to his skin. She could make out the taut muscles of his upper arms, the tight wall of his chest through the saturated silk.

Quickly she averted her gaze.

"I'm fine." She pushed back the hair that hung like rat's tails over her face. "I can't believe how quickly that came out of nowhere."

"Aziz is a desert town, this is a desert thunderstorm."

Already the forecourt was under water, Jayne stared at the sheer volume of water that rushed down the steep slope of the road in disbelief. She could barely make out the shape of the limousine through the thick, grey veil of the rain.

"How long will this last?"

Tariq shrugged. "Not long enough."

"Not long enough?" Jayne stared with disbelief at angry torrent of water rushing below the step where she was standing. "You want *more* of this?"

"Look past the destruction." He gestured beyond the rain. "There lies the desert where water is life. A cloudburst is cause for celebration, even though it will bring grief, too. That's the desert way."

"It's hard."

"Inshallah."

"How can you simply accept it? Just like that?"

"Breathe deeply."

"What?" She started at him blankly.

"Close your eyes and breathe deeply," he ordered.

"Why?"

"Do it and it will become clear."

Jayne closed her eyes and inhaled. "Like that?"

"What can you smell?"

She concentrated. "Wet. The fresh, steaming scent of rain."

"What else? What is missing?"

She opened her eyes. "Dust. The arid desert dust."

"Yes." He grinned down at her. "The rain is wonderful. It

washes away the dust and brings green and life. And, for a few days, there will be a fresh scent to the whole world before the dust and dryness returns for the rest of the year."

Jayne stared at the sheets of rain hammering down and gushing down the hill. "Where will all that go?"

"The city is ancient, and rain water was not a priority for the creators. The water will sit in large flat puddles on the surface until it evaporates. There is little vegetation in the desert to absorb the rain, so dry wadis will become rivers."

Jayne shook her head, and droplets scattered. She gave a little shiver as a wind gusted up the hill to where they stood under the overhang. The limousine had long since been driven away to the garages. The world felt utterly deserted except for the two of them. Ahead the sheets of rain obscured the view down the hill to the town on the one side and the stretching desert to the other.

"You are very wet. You need to change." Tariq's gaze lingered on the front of her dress, making her very aware of the way the sodden fabric clung to her breasts and how the cold wind had caused the tight nubs to jut out. She folded her arms and shivered.

"You need to change, too."

Thirty minutes later Tariq strode swiftly down the corridor, frowning a little as he took in the dingy darkness in the wing where he'd been told his sheikhah's room was located. No doubt this must be a quieter wing of the fort. He rounded a corner and stopped at the third door on the left. Raising his hand, he rapped three times. It opened a crack, and Jayne peered around the door at him.

"Yes?"

She didn't sound at all welcoming. He took in her damp

hair, the loose diaphanous caftan that covered her from head to toe, only the open neckline revealing that her skin was still damp from her bath.

"You were wet and cold, I wanted to see that you were okay."

That was his first excuse for being here.

Her expression told him she wasn't buying it. "I'm fine, a little water won't harm me. What do you want, Tariq?"

He tried the next excuse. "We will not be able to leave tomorrow. Floods have washed away the desert road! I have summoned the royal helicopter. But every helicopter in the country is busy with emergency missions in the wake of the cloudburst. I did not feel it right to divert them—not while there are people in need."

Now she looked a little less suspicious. "But what about your father…?"

"He is feeling much better. I spoke to him, too." Tariq moved a little closer. His father had told him to take time to get to know his wife, to become friends…lovers. Not to hurry back. "He knows we are stranded here for a few days. He told me to take my time, to do what needs to be done."

"How close are you to a resolution with Sheikh Karim?"

"It should not take much longer."

But he had not sought her out to speak about politics. He couldn't forget the look on her face when he'd challenged her that she'd believed he'd broken his wedding vows while they were together. Why had he never sensed how alienated she must have felt? He searched her eyes trying to read what lay behind the wariness with which she regarded him. "Let me in, we need to talk."

But still she did not open the door. Instead bit her lip and said, "What's there to talk about?"

He fixed his gaze on the spot where her white teeth played with her lip, the endearing little gap between her front teeth. He had a sudden wild urge to put his mouth, his tongue, exactly *there.* He glanced away before the impulse overtook him. "About the fact that you believed that I was incapable of remaining true to you—only you."

She gave an exasperated sigh and started to close the door on him. "Tariq, it's *years* too late for this discussion."

"Maybe not." He pushed it back, leaning forward against the solid wood. "I've only today learned of your irrational concerns about other women."

"Irrational?" Jayne stepped back, and the door flew open.

He brushed past her, and stopped dead. "*What the hell is this?* Is this where you have been sleeping?"

"Yes."

"In this hole?"

She nodded wordlessly.

He reached for her hand. "Come, we are leaving."

"I thought you said we couldn't leave yet."

He gave an impatient mutter. "We can't leave the town, but we can find accommodation elsewhere in the town." He pulled her toward him. "Ali has insulted me."

Oh, no. She could see the hard work of the negotiation all going up in smoke. "Tariq, wait. I doubt he even knows. This is Leila's doing, not Ali's, I'm sure of it. Ignore it. Don't let Leila cause more trouble than already exists."

"You are my wife." There was a white ring around his mouth. "There is respect due to you."

"How can you expect others to respect me when you don't?"

He looked at her, stark shock showing in his eyes, and then he got it under control, shuttering his reaction from her scrutiny. "What you ask is too much. The evidence against you was too heavy. *There was a child.*"

Jayne sagged. "It would never have worked anyway."

He caught her hand. The bones stood out beneath his skin, stretching it taut. "Do you know what the worst of it is?" His voice was low, tormented. "I still want you. Despite everything."

She knew what the admission must have cost him.

But it wasn't enough.

"I thought I could control this insanity. But when I saw you outside, your clothes clinging to your body—" he lifted his hand and cupped her breast "—every curve revealed, I wanted you. I'm surrendering. I can no longer resist."

"Tariq!"

But it was too late. His head was already lowering. His mouth closed over hers. For a moment she wanted to object. She should not be allowing this….

His tongue stroked across the seam of her lips…gently… tenderly. Emotion gushed through her. With a soft sigh, she relented and her lips parted.

One kiss.

Just one kiss.

But one turned to two. Then three. Then his mouth trailed a row of heated kisses along her neck.

"Tariq." This time it was a sigh of concession.

He pulled her closer, crushing her against him, and kissed her deeply, driving her wild. His lean length pressed against her, until a fierce tension vibrated through her. She threaded her hands through his hair, loving the soft silkiness between her fingers.

He moaned, a harsh, guttural sound. Then he raised his head. "I am not making love to you in this rat hole. Come with me."

Jayne went, dragged along by this devastating force that raged between them. Unseen, they hurried along the labyrinth of twists and turns until they reached his bedchamber.

Jayne caught a glimpse of the dark turbulent skies through the open latticed shutters, then Tariq kicked the door shut and yanked her back into his arms.

"I want you," he muttered.

Shivers chased down her spine at the raw need in his voice.

"Tell me you want me, Jayne."

For a moment she resisted. Boy, he could have any woman he crooked his little finger at. Why did he need her reassurance?

He hauled her closer. *"Tell me."*

His hardness pressed against her, leaving her in no doubt about the extent of his need.

In a low tone she admitted, "I want you, too."

"Good," he purred. "I want there to be no doubt about that later. No regrets."

No regrets? For a second she froze, almost pulled back. But then he swept her up, carried her to the bed and laid her down on the covers. She opened her mouth, glanced up at him…and all her thoughts flew out her head at the look in his eyes.

Hot.

Tender.

Almost…loving…? No, not loving, it was too intense, too carnal.

But it shook her to her soul. For a moment she felt an ache at the closeness she'd missed in the years they had spent apart. Then she excised it ruthlessly. Need—even love—was worth nothing without trust.

And he hadn't—still didn't—trust her.

So what the hell was she doing in his bed?

Seeking pleasure…seeking the completion only Tariq had ever given her. She moaned at the realisation. And Tariq took it for a moan of passion and reared back.

"You feel it, too?" His eyes blazed with joy.

How could she kill that?

Instead she nodded, biting her lip. The shutter at the window banged, caught by a gust of wind. She jumped.

"Hush," he murmured. "Everything will be right."

Not everything.

Not ever.

She shut her eyes against the sudden intrusion. His lips brushed her eyelids. Soft, butterfly kisses. Then his hands were sliding down her body, parting the front of the lacy silk of the caftan, pushing it off her shoulders, down her arms. A brief fumble with the clasp, then her bra was gone, leaving only high-cut briefs.

She waited, eyes still shut.

But the touch she expected did not come. Instead she heard the rustle of fabric. Her eyes flickered open. The white *thobe* he'd worn lay on the floor. All that remained were a pair of snug boxer briefs that hugged every bulge.

She blinked. "Goodness."

"It will be good," he growled, unsmilingly. And his eyes caught fire as he reached for her.

Her heart went into overdrive. His fingers closed on her shoulders, bringing her close. Her skin felt hot under his cool touch. The shutter slammed again, and a blast of wind blew into the bedchamber.

"Wait, I will be back in a moment."

Tariq got off the bed and crossed the room to fasten the shutters. Then he turned. For an instant he stood, proud, powerful.

Jayne could see the arrogance from generations of Emirs instilled in him. In the tilt of his head. In the sureness of his stance.

He bent down, pushing the briefs along his legs, then he was moving toward her, tall and straight.

And utterly naked.

For a moment she forgot to breathe.

He was beautiful.

The covers gave as he landed on the bed beside her. He touched her and she quivered. Waiting…

He kissed her. Until she was breathless. Before she could recover, his fingers slipped under the elastic of her briefs and slid them away. Tariq moved over her, his skin like silk against hers. Propping his elbows on either side of her arms, he gazed down at her. The golden eyes were hot and fierce.

"It has been far too long. I am not sure if I can hold."

Her eyes stretched wide. "Tariq?"

"We will take it slowly. Very slowly."

It sounded like a promise.

His fingers slid between them, he cupped her breast, then bent his head and tongued the pebbled tip. Her body responded, arching eagerly beneath him. His tongue touched her again.

Jayne gasped and closed her eyes.

Under her fingertips the slick silk of the bedcover felt unbearably sensual. Tariq shifted. His fingertips trailed down her body…over her belly…exploring the changes.

For a moment Jayne stiffened. A stab of loss shook her as his palm smoothed over her flat stomach. Was he thinking of the life that had once lain there? She sighed. No, he was probably doing everything in his power to forget it.

"Don't sound so sad, *habiibtii*. It will be good."

His words gave her pause. "Even if it is good. We should not be doing this." It was a whisper, but even against the whistling wind he heard it.

He raised his head and met her gaze squarely. But she read defiance in his eyes.

"Why not?" he demanded.

"Because we are getting divorced!"

Something flashed in his eyes. Then it was gone. "There is nothing wrong with making love. We are married, you are my wife. There is no sin in this."

"But there is no love, either," Jayne retorted, her ardour cooling a little.

"What is love?" Tariq's rough voice echoed in the bed-chamber. "We had love in the past and it was not enough."

Oh, what was the use?

He thought it hadn't worked because she'd found someone else. It hadn't worked for her because she'd needed his complete trust. Between them had stood the Emir, who held the alleged evidence of her adultery, the father who Tariq trusted with his life.

She got nowhere arguing with Tariq. And falling into bed with her husband was an even worse idea.

"Let me up." She tried to sit up, wanting to dress…cover herself. His hand stroked her stomach, moving lower. She shuddered as desire ignited in places she'd thought the embers long cold. "Let me up."

"Are you sure you want to get up, walk out that door? Never experience this fierce pleasure again?"

She hesitated.

"What do you say, *nuur il-en?* Light of my eyes?"

Light of his eyes. She stared into the gold flame of his gaze and all will to fight dissipated. Tariq read her surrender and growled, a hoarse, hungry sound.

"Is this what you want?" His mouth was all over her. Her body shuddered. She couldn't speak, she could only feel… and feel…and feel.

"Tell me," he demanded. "Do you want more? Or do you want me to stop?" His mouth ravaged the soft flesh of her belly, moving lower. She groaned again.

"What did you say?"

"Yes!" she burst out.

His lean, powerful body froze against hers. "You want me to stop."

"No, damn you." She was almost sobbing now. She reached for him, her hands knotting in his hair. "I want you to…" Her voice trailed away.

He held her off. "To what?"

"I want you to—" rage flashed through her, heated by desire "—I want you to make love to me. Now!"

"Good." He smiled, a hard ruthless curve of his lips. "I'm glad we've got that clear."

This time he touched her with purpose. No more teasing now. He was in control. She felt it in the stroke of his hand. Total mastery. Nothing less.

His fingers caressed her most secret places, causing her to gasp out loud. He touched again. This time she almost came apart.

"I can't." She bit her lip…fighting…fighting the waves of pleasure that threatened to crash over her and sweep her away. "What about you?"

"Don't worry about me." He gave her a wild, reckless grin. "I won't take long, *habiibtii*. Not tonight."

Then his hips fitted into the cradle of hers. He plunged forward. Jayne gasped as he slid all the way forward, sheathing himself deep within her.

Involuntarily her hips lifted. This time Tariq lost his breath in a husky moan. He started to move. Jayne reached for him, her fingers pressing into his spine.

"*Habiibtii,* if you do that it's going to be over before we've started," he whispered hotly in her ear. "So don't touch me—or it will be past."

She dropped her hands, clutched the silk cover.

Tariq pulled back, slid in. Then repeated the motion. The friction was slow and sensual and utterly delicious. Jayne felt the half-forgotten tension spiraling within her, tighter and tighter, as he continued to move. Until finally something gave, deep in the core of her, and the ripples started.

Tariq moaned. "Hold me."

Her arms came around him, pulling him close. And then his breathing became ragged and his body jerked in her arms.

"Do you know why I find you beautiful?"

It was past midnight. Outside the wind had died. The golden glow of light from the bedside table cast a warm hue on the walls and on Tariq's skin where he lay, head propped on his arm as he watched her.

A lump filled Jayne's throat. She shook her head.

"From that first time I saw you in the Tate Gallery, I

couldn't take my eyes off you. You glowed with serenity. You still do. Your skin has the radiance of the most prized Gulf pearls, your hair has the gloss of the sun on a raven's wing. When I touch your skin, your hair, it feels like silk."

"I'm not—"

"Beautiful? Don't tell me that! Whose standards do you judge yourself against? The magazines? Hollywood?" He shook his head. "They are of no import to me. There are many kinds of beauty…and to me you are beautiful."

The romanticism of his words swept her breath away.

She thought of Neil's advice that she cut her hair short. It suited her new studies, he said, her new career path as a departmental head of literacy studies. Short hair would look far more professional than her fly-away locks.

But she didn't want to feel professional. She wanted to feel feminine…desired…beautiful.

And that's what Tariq had achieved.

He made her feel alive. She stretched a hand out toward him.

"Wait, I have something for you." He leapt from the bed and rummaged through his clothes. A moment later he was back holding the satin bag from the gold *souq*.

"Tariq—"

"Don't refuse." He drew out the ankle chain she had admired. The little bells tinkled. Lifting her leg, he stroked it and fastened the chain around her ankle.

She started to object.

"Hush." He bent forward and placed a kiss against the soft skin beside her ankle bone.

Just as her pulse started to quicken, he straightened and his hand disappeared back into the bag. This time it emerged with a necklace. A circlet of gold threaded with large beads made of amber and turquoise.

"I can't accept that." The amber was the same colour as his eyes. Her heart ached. She didn't want gifts of gold. Yet he would never give her what she most wanted. His trust. "It's too valuable."

"Look on it as protection from any evil." His lips twisted. "To keep you safe. All the days of your life."

"Oh, Tariq." Her heart turned over. This was no ingot intended to buy his way into her heart. This was a farewell gift. Something to remember him by when it was all over. But she knew that she would never forget him, how could she? When part of him remained with her, every day of her life?

"May there always be a road for you, *nuur il-en,* and may it always be blessed. Now lean forward so that I can fasten this."

She obeyed.

He lifted her hair, and his fingers fumbled for a moment as he did up the clasp. His lips brushed her neck, then he was kissing her neck and shivers of desire swept her. Jayne turned in his arms and lifted her face. When the kiss came, it burned with suppressed passion.

She groaned and reached for him, closing her arms around him.

Tariq was late getting to his meeting with Karim the following morning. He drifted into the formal meeting room in a daze, still reeling under the passion of the long night.

"Sabah al-hayri," Karim greeted him.

Tariq pulled himself together. It would not do to look like a love-struck youth to his powerful neighbour. "Good morning," he returned.

But his mind kept straying from the negotiations. To visions of Jayne draped across his chest, her smile warm and sensual. To the memory of the silkiness of her skin under his fingertips.

"Tariq?"

He gave a start. Karim was staring at him, wearing a bemused expression.

"What do you think?"

What did he think? He blinked. He could hardly confess that he thought he should be in bed with his wife.

Karim was trying to be reasonable. For the first time in days Tariq had lost all interest in the settlement. He longed for his wife's arms…to forget the mess that his father's comrades had landed him in. More than anything he wanted to put an end to this internecine bickering and return to Jayne.

"What about I include that spur of land on the sea that lies on the Zayedi side of the border to apologise for the shame my kinsmen have caused you, Karim?"

Karim was frowning. "Let's not bring land into it. The last time land was promised to me by your family the deal was dishonoured."

"By whom?" Tariq shook his head to clear it and leaned forward, his elbows on the table.

"Your father."

A hot rush of anger followed Karim's accusation. All languor left him. "Don't lie. The Emir would never dishonour a deal."

Karim rose to his feet. "If you are going to call me a liar, then our business is done." He picked up his jacket.

"Wait." Karim was not the kind of man to cast stones at a dying man. Tariq bit back his rage and tried hard for a conciliatory tone. "You must understand, my father is a man of honour and he is—" Tariq broke off and swallowed "—very ill. Your statement hit a nerve."

Karim paused at the door.

Tariq took a deep breath and tried again. "Give me more details. Please. I need to investigate this." This must be a misunderstanding. His father would never break his word. Would never do anything underhand. Tariq would track down where the misunderstanding lay. And then he would deal with it.

"His Highest Excellency promised me a tract of land to extend the wetlands that we are building in Bashir." Karim's lips curved into a hard smile. "Ironically, they are not far from the spur of land you now offer me."

"I have heard talk of the gift." Karim's commitment to creating wetlands was well-known. It would have been the kind of thing his father might have done to better relations. Give a piece of marshland with not much value and receive a wealth of gratitude and goodwill in return.

"The gift was never made." Karim's jade eyes glittered. "Ali discovered oil there and persuaded your father to lease the lands to him."

"I know nothing of the discovery of any oil in that part of the country." Bewildered, Tariq stared at the other sheikh. "This cannot be true."

"Then there is nothing more to be said." Karim's hand reached for the door handle.

"Don't go." Tariq felt a burning behind his eyes. He didn't want to lose Karim's friendship. They'd played together as children in the Bedu camps and become firm friends as men. But it was important not to back down. This was a matter of honour. His family's honour. Yet Karim clearly believed what he said to be true. So to placate him Tariq said, "By Allah, if I find there has been dishonour, you will be gifted those lands, too."

He made the vow, comfortable that he wouldn't find anything like that. But he couldn't afford to alienate Karim. Too much depended on it.

There was something curiously like sadness in Karim's eyes. Pity? No, it couldn't be pity. Tariq shook his head to free himself of the notion.

"Tariq?" Karim's voice was low and very grave. "Arranging a marriage between you and Yasmin was an attempt to demolish the wall that was rising between Bashir and Zayed. Don't be too hard on your father when you get to the bottom of it. He is dying…don't spoil this last time by chastising him. He is only a man. Let him go to the afterlife at peace."

"My father is much more than an ordinary man, he is the Emir of Zayed." Karim didn't know what he was talking about. Even Jayne had come to realise that he would hear no criticism of his father. Soon he would have to step into his father's mighty shoes and he would be the Emir of Zayed.

But first he needed to convince himself that his father was at peace. That he would die fulfilled.

Shortly afterwards, Tariq shook hands with Karim and, after the other man's departure, he reached for his cell phone and dialled a number that he had never had cause to call.

Ten

The next couple of days passed in a haze.

Tariq spent most of his days in meetings with Mahood and Ali and Karim, but he'd told Jayne that a resolution was imminent. She lived from day to day, trying not to think about the future…or the past.

In the evenings Ali and his brother hosted elaborate state dinners with all kinds of entertainment provided. Singers. Dancers. But it was for the nights that Jayne lived. Nights spent clandestinely making love with her husband.

Jayne insisted on returning to her poky little room in the early hours of each morning and mussing the bed. Soon she and Tariq would be divorced. She needed to keep some sort of separation in her own mind. So she worked hard to maintain the fiction that they occupied separate rooms. It was difficult to think beyond the nights when they scorched the sheets before parting in the morning.

Their marriage was over, killed long ago by his distrust. But there was no reason why she couldn't make love with her husband. What damage could be done? And who would ever know?

That evening, the reception rooms downstairs were packed with people who had come to see the sheikh. Jayne watched as he was accosted and asked for advice.

"Sheikh Tariq is a master falconer. The kind of man who takes what he has learned in the desert and applies it to his leadership. He is wise, patient. He will be a worthy Emir."

Jayne started at the sound of Sheikh Karim's low voice. Every word only highlighted the difference between her and Tariq. Looking up at him she said, "If I'd known who he was when I met him, I would never have married him."

Karim raised an eyebrow. "Perhaps that is why he never told you."

"What do you mean?"

"He is a man capable of great passion. If only he could take the emotion he shares with his falcons and apply them to the people around him. He is more relaxed when you are around. When you are out of his sight he is restless, like a man who is incomplete."

"He doesn't need me."

"He needs you more than you might think. Why else has he never remarried? There has been enough opportunity."

Jayne felt her hackles rise. "He needs to divorce me first."

"Have you ever asked yourself why he has never done so?" Karim's smile was rueful when Jayne slowly shook her head. "Perhaps you should."

Jayne was still thinking about Karim's words when she crossed the cavernous entrance hall and made her way to the powder room. Why had Tariq never divorced her and remarried? Frowning, she pushed the door open and came to a halt.

Leila stood in front of the mirror, applying *kajal* around her dark eyes. Jayne hesitated, tempted to turn and run. Then she straightened her spine and stepped forward.

Without looking at the other woman, Jayne poured herself a glass of water from the tall ceramic jar that stood on the table and drank it down. Then she opened her bag, searching for a tissue.

A sound made her turn. Leila stood beside her, her lips curled back in a snarl. "You don't have what it takes to keep a man like Sheikh Tariq."

How was she supposed to respond to that?

Jayne decided to ignore her. She zipped up her bag and started toward the door.

"You are running away. Soon you will leave here and I will get Tariq."

Jayne paused at the door. "You are delusional. Tariq would never touch another man's wife."

Leila's face turned ugly. "I am divorcing my husband. And my father will make it part of these settlement negotiations that Tariq marry me—otherwise there will be war between Zayed and Bashir."

"That's not going to happen." Jayne had heard enough. Leila was a spoiled little witch who deserved to be taken down a peg. She turned the handle. "In terms of our marriage contract, Tariq has promised not to marry another woman while he is married to me. And I will *never* divorce him."

Why on earth had she said that? Jayne was still reeling from the surprise of hearing her own words when Leila gave a growl of fury and rushed at her, hands clawing at the air, eyes glittering with malice.

Jayne ducked. Too late. A painful stinging sensation slashed down her cheek. Jayne cried out and pushed the door, nearly falling into the corridor outside.

"Jayne." Tariq's hands caught her shoulders, steadying her.

She heard his breath catch. "You are bleeding. These are scratch marks. Who did this to you?" The sheer anger in his voice was overwhelming.

"Tariq—"

The door behind her opened and Leila stepped out. Tariq's fingers tightened on Jayne's skin and he pulled her close. His body was warm against hers, but she could feel the tightly coiled tension in his muscles.

"You have hurt the sheikhah."

Leila's eyes widened at the cold rage in the accusation. "I didn't—"

"Do not lie to me." Fury vibrated through each word. "You will be punished for this transgression."

"Please, no." Leila fell to her knees at his feet, bowing her head and grabbing at the hem of his *thobe*. "Don't you understand? I did it for you. *For us.*"

Tariq stared down at her. "Get up."

Jayne shivered at the icy tone.

"I have left my husband, we are getting divorced, so that I can marry you."

"What are you talking about?" Stunned amazement replaced his anger.

Leila raised her head. "I was always meant to be your wife. Not her. It will be made right. My father intends to speak to you."

"For the sake of Allah, can you not understand?" Jayne

shuddered at the impatience in Tariq's voice and buried her face in the soft fabric that covered his chest. "I already have a wife—I do not want another. I saw you watching me earlier, Leila. You are to visit the doctor, you need help. You will do so tomorrow. Agreed?" Tariq's voice had gentled but a core of steel remained. Jayne raised her head in time to see Leila nod and stumble to her feet.

Tariq held Jayne tightly to him. "Now I am taking my wife to tend to her hurts, and you will not threaten her again, ever."

A sense of wonder filled Jayne at his heated defence of her. A protective Tariq was almost impossible to resist.

That night Tariq's lovemaking was exquisitely gentle.

At first he touched her with fingers that were almost reverent, as if she were fragile and something infinitely precious. But slowly as the heat mounted, his hands ignited a wild response. Where he touched, fire followed.

The soft, devout kisses became hot sweeps of his tongue. Jayne twisted on the bed, her body stretched out, at the mercy of his loving.

It was wild. It was unfettered. It held a sweetness that had been lacking previously.

"Mine," he declared as his body thrust into hers, claiming her. *Mine.*

It echoed through Jayne's head as she started to move with him, under him, eager for the shivers of desire to engulf them both. When the moment came, Jayne cried out.

Tariq hugged her close to him, holding her tight, his body shaking with the force of their lovemaking.

And for the first time, Jayne wondered whether she could walk away from the man who had claimed her heart.

* * *

"So much for a three-day absence from the palace," Jayne said the next morning as they dressed hurriedly. They had both overslept. Jayne had wakened to find her limbs entangled with Tariq's and the sun already well up.

Tariq touched her face and stared at her with hot eyes. "The contretemps with Leila aside, would you have missed one minute of what we have shared?"

Slowly Jayne shook her head. "But I can't help worrying about your father. I don't want you one day to regret this time, because it cost you time with your father."

"I have spoken to him several times every day. He is in better spirits than he has been for a long time. But we should be able to leave tomorrow. The helicopter has dealt with the worst of the disasters caused by the rains."

Unexpectedly Jayne's heart sank at the thought of leaving here.

"If you'll excuse me, there's a call I need to make," Tariq said.

A little hurt at his brusque tone, Jayne flounced to the door. "I'd better start to pack." She left Tariq fingering his phone, checking on his father.

They left the following morning. As the helicopter rose, Noor gave a sharp squawk of protest from her *kafas,* and a sudden pang of sorrow shook Jayne. This time in Aziz had been so precious. Careful not to let Tariq see her face, she leaned forward to look out the window. Far below, the sun glinted off the silver pools where the town still lay under water. They flew over the desert and she peered down through the windows with disbelief. It had only been a couple of days since they'd travelled across the dry desert but already the desertscape had changed. Down below Jayne could see a sprinkling of green across the desert.

"It's the rain," Tariq said, pointing below. "The wildflowers will be blossoming, too. As soon as it rains everything comes to life."

The rains might bring life to the desert…but there was nothing that could bring their marriage to life. It had been doomed before it had ever started. Jayne swallowed. And, when it had ended, she'd had to make a choice that Tariq would never forgive.

If he ever found out…she shivered. She did not want to think about what might happen.

By noon they were back at the palace.

Tariq disappeared to visit his father and, left alone, Jayne made her way slowly back to her boudoir. Why had she expected anything to have changed with their renewed… closeness? Tariq was still a sheikh, a traditional male, and she would always take second place to his family…his political business.

And it wasn't as if she were back permanently, as his real wife. *They were getting divorced.* She had to stop thinking like a wife. But it was hard. Making love to him had bared emotions she'd never expected to feel again.

Not expecting to see him for the rest of the day, she retreated to the library, to the valuable collection of books housed there. Latifa found her there. She brought a cup of jasmine tea and some sweets, and Jayne heard how overjoyed the Emir had been by the return of his son.

There was relief in the younger woman's eyes. Jayne realised that she had not been alone in her fear that the Emir might pass from this world while Tariq was away settling Ali and Mahood's disputes.

By midafternoon Tariq was still not back, so Jayne settled down in Tariq's study and booted up his computer. She owed Samantha some information on Zayed, for her school project. She would ask Tariq for some photos to e-mail tonight.

There were e-mails from Helen waiting for her. Concerned e-mails. Her sister had seen the news about the floods in Zayed on television and the rescue efforts. She had tried to ring Jayne on her cell phone but hadn't gotten through. There was a photo, too, of Amy's first day at school. Amy looked so grown-up. So confident.

Jayne's throat tightened.

How she missed them all.

In the end, Jayne picked up the phone and dialled Auckland. It was good to talk to her sister and the girls. Curiously calming. By the time she said her farewells, she no longer felt as lonely as she had with Tariq busy with the affairs of state.

While Tariq divided his time between his father's sick bed and listening to the petitions of the citizens of Zayed who came from near and far each day, Jayne found herself spending more and more time in the raptor mews with the young saker falcon called Haytham that Tariq intended to release into the wild at the end of the season.

She was feeding the bird titbits when she received a visitor one morning.

"Sabah al-hayri," her visitor greeted.

"Good morning, Dr. Jirah." Brushing off her hands, Jayne

took off the glove and walked toward the woman with whom she'd chatted at the banquet what seemed an aeon ago.

"Kef Halak?"

Jayne paused. *"Ma atakallam arabi."* She stumbled over the words. "I'm sorry, but I don't speak Arabic."

"The correct response to my question, which meant 'How are you', is *zein al-Hamdulillah,* 'Fine thanks,'" said the doctor. "I am aware that you don't speak our language, but don't you think that if you are interested in falconry, in the Bedu roots from where the Emirs of Zayed originate, then, my dear, the time has come to learn to speak your husband's language?"

How on earth should she respond to the doctor's unusual frankness? Obviously, she couldn't confess that she and Tariq would be divorced in the near future—although the date of that event was becoming less and less important to Jayne.

Better to take refuge in half truths buried far in the past. "I tried to learn when I was here previously, but it was a struggle. And I never expected that we would stay in Zayed for long." She'd been so clueless. It had taken a while for it to dawn that Tariq was expected to succeed his father as Emir. There would be no life as a young married couple in London, raising children in a village a commutable distance from the city. And then there had been the difficulty in securing someone to teach her Arabic. No one had appeared to want to risk the Emir's displeasure by consorting with the daughter-in-law he despised.

Jayne had been an outcast.

And Tariq had been too busy to see it.

She'd had no friends, no social support network, and her husband had never been home.

He'd been sent on mission after mission, to neighbouring

Gulf states, to Europe, on political deputations. She'd been left in Zayed, alone and isolated and increasingly unhappy.

The only person who had talked to her had been Roger, the English book restorer charged with tending the Emir's library. And in the end that miserly friendship had cost Jayne her marriage.

How to explain that to the woman facing her?

"I heard you tried to learn a little and then you gave up at the first obstacle."

"I didn't speak well. I embarrassed the Emir with my pidgin Arabic."

Farrah waved her hands. "Who cares about the Emir—it is your husband you should be concerned with. It doesn't matter how you speak, at least be able to talk and understand a little—even if it is pidgin Arabic. It shows goodwill and soon you will make female friends who will help you learn—like I can."

"You would do that?"

"Of course. That's why I am here." The doctor gave her a smile. "And I have another agenda. But we will discuss that later."

"I couldn't speak. So when Tariq wasn't here, I started to refuse any invitations to go out and they tapered off."

"Not because your company wasn't wanted. But once you'd refused, no one wanted to put you in the embarrassing position of having to refuse again. To refuse two invitations is rude, and no one wanted to put you in that awkward place."

"Oh." That put a whole different complexion on it. She'd thought that everyone despised her. Boy, she'd been so young. So naive.

"It helps to have a hobby, too, one that keeps you busy

while the men talk and expect you to spend the evening with the other wives."

"What do you do?" Jayne asked with interest.

"I knit booties for the babies I deliver. There are lots of those." She smiled. "Sometimes the company can be very boring. That is why I hoped you and I could be friends."

"Where were you when I was here last?" Jayne complained. If only she had met this forthright woman then.

"Working in a hospital in London, completing my training."

"I'll think of something that would be better than twiddling my thumbs. I've always wanted to learn to do cross-stitch." Jayne could not tell her new friend that she would not be here to see the friendship through.

"Good," Farrah said briskly. "Now to the other reason I am here. I hear that you are interested in literacy."

"How did you hear that?"

Farrah smiled sphinxlike. "From a patient."

Dexter, the tall Texan. It had to be. Jayne tipped her head sideways and studied the doctor. "Do I detect a romance?"

"Perhaps. But it will take time and work to see if it will last."

Jayne envied Farrah her composure, her levelheaded approach. "I wish you luck."

"Thank you. Now back to my request about literacy."

When Farrah left, Jayne shook her hand and said a heartfelt, *"Shukran."* Thank you.

That evening Jayne and Tariq had settled down to search for photos to send to Samantha for her school project when a knock sounded on the door. Hadi al Ebrahim, the Emir's trusted aide, stood there looking very grave. "Excellency," he addressed Tariq. "There is a problem."

"My father!" Tariq was on his feet in one swift move.

"No." Hadi cast a glance at Jayne. "It is about the divorce, Excellency."

Apprehension tied Jayne's stomach up into knots. "What about the divorce?" she demanded.

Hadi gave Tariq a hunted look. "Can we discuss this privately?"

"This concerns me. The divorce is the reason I am here in Zayed." She voiced her worst fears, "Is something wrong?"

"There are rumours, Excellency," Hadi said delicately.

"What kind of rumours?" Tariq's brows drew low over his eyes.

"That you and the sheikhah shared accommodation."

Jayne shot Tariq a furtive glance. She flushed slightly as she remembered those steamy illicit nights they'd spent together in the fort at Aziz. Had someone seen her returning to her room in the early hours of the morning? Was that what this was about?

"We had separate rooms in Aziz," Jayne told Hadi. "But why is this important?" She shut out the thought that while they might have had separate rooms, they'd spent the nights in each other's arms.

"Not at Aziz," Wadi replied. "In the Bedu camp. It is said you shared a tent."

"So?" Jayne started to get annoyed. Tariq might be a sheikh but why did she have to face this invasion of her private life. "We're married. I've committed no sin. Even if we did share the tent, what does it matter?"

"Jayne—"

"What?" she turned on Tariq. "Why does this matter—"

"It matters." Tariq's face was expressionless.

Jayne stilled. She glanced rapidly from one man to the other. "What's going on? Why is this so important?"

"Jayne, listen to me—"

"No, I want to hear it from Hadi." She swung around. "Hadi, what's going on?"

The older man looked extremely uncomfortable.

"Tell me."

At last he said, "Sheikhah, under the laws of Zayed, a husband and wife need to live apart for five years to be granted a divorce."

"But we have lived apart for five years."

"Sheikhah, the night in the desert nullifies those years."

"What?" Jayne stared at him in horror. "How can it?"

"What Hadi is trying to say is that under our laws the couple need to stay apart for five years before they can be granted a divorce. If they spend the night under the same roof there is a presumption that they've had sexual relations, which would need to be disproved."

"But we didn't sleep together in the desert."

Hadi gave a cough of discomfort. "Then the sheikh and sheikhah have no problems. They simply apply to court and state on oath they have not shared—" he swallowed audibly "—sexual relations for the past five years."

Horror filled Jayne. How could she swear such an oath? It would be a lie. She glanced at Tariq. His face was blank, utterly expressionless.

"Hadi, thank you, you may go now." It was a dismissal.

"Thank you, Excellency." He bowed and walked backward to the great double doors. "The Emir will be saddened that the divorce is going ahead. He had such high hopes for this desert trip."

"You are not to say a word to him about the divorce," Tariq warned, his eyes hard.

When the door shut, Jayne turned on him. "You knew about this five-year provision?" Tariq nodded. Her brain started to click over. She remembered the night in his bed-chamber. He'd just spoken to his father. He'd told her the Emir was feeling better. Had he been prepared to go to these lengths for his father's sake, to ensure his father died a happy man?

Was that why he'd made love to her?

"Jayne—"

"Don't talk to me. I'm thinking."

"Jayne, don't jump to conclusions—"

"You planned this," Jayne hissed. "You wanted to keep me trapped in Zayed."

Angry colour flooded his cheeks. "Why would I plan this?"

"Because this is what your father wanted—and you have always done what your father wants. You are a puppet on a string, Tariq."

His eyes flashed. "Watch what you say, wife. Why would I want you to stay? You hate this place—"

"I started to like—"

Tariq talked straight over her attempt to tell him that she'd changed her mind about the desert. "Why would I *want* a wife I can never trust near another man?"

Jayne gave a snort of disgust. "The old double standard. You are surrounded by temptation every day, yet you assure me you have never strayed. I believe you. Why can't you believe me?"

"*Because I have my father's word.* He saw you kissing Roger with his own eyes, caught you naked in the library."

"That's utter rubbish. I told you before."

Tariq's looked utterly tormented. "How can I not believe my father? He's a man of honour, the Emir of Zayed!"

"And I am your wife!"

"That would mean…"

She could see him thinking it through. She nodded. "Yes, the child I carried was yours, Tariq."

"No, that is not true." He shook his head. "My father would never lie. He told me it was Roger's child."

"So I'm the liar?"

Tariq raised his head and stared at her oppressively. "But what does it matter? The child is gone, there is nothing more to discuss."

"Except the end of our marriage." Tariq didn't answer her. She huffed out a heavy sigh. "And now I'm trapped for another five years in a marriage I no longer want. But you can't stop me leaving. Even if I can't have my divorce, I will not stay."

"Not until my father dies."

"Or the month is up. Whichever comes first. And then I want your promise that you will not come near me for five years."

"And what if I can't give you that, *habiibtii?*" Tariq's eyes were dark with some emotion that looked curiously like pain.

Jayne stared at him, at a total loss for words.

Eleven

Jayne was still angry and confused when she went down to the mews to visit Haytham, the young saker falcon the next morning. How could she have been stupid enough to have slept with Tariq in Aziz? She'd come to Zayed to get a divorce so that she could get on with her life and cut the ties with the past—and Tariq.

She kicked a stone off the path in front of the mews. Now it would be another five years before she could get a divorce. A memory of Tariq kissing her…of his hands lingering on her body…flashed through her mind. Images shifted like a kaleidoscope. Tariq drinking coffee and laughing. Tariq making love to her, his eyes burning.

Did she really want a divorce?

But how could she stay married to a man who didn't trust her? She'd planned a whole new life in Auckland, how could she throw it all away and come back to Zayed? And would Tariq even want her back?

Her head spinning, she entered the raptor mews and came to an abrupt stop at the sight of Tariq.

He stood beside Noor's empty perch, tall and commanding even in a pair of light coloured casual pants and a white T-shirt. Noor rode on the *mangalah* strapped to his arm to stop her claws damaging skin. With a hood over her head and a leash securing the jesses to the glove, it was clear that Tariq was taking her out to fly.

The falcon's feathers were pulled tight in anticipation and her head turned to the doorway where Jayne stood.

"You say you want to learn to fly a falcon. I'm going to exercise Noor with the lure. Do you want to come?"

Jayne nodded. But she knew that once she returned to Auckland she would give up that idea. It simply wouldn't work. It was another mirage.

They walked out to a flat piece of parkland behind the mews, surrounded by hedges and planted with tall date palms.

Tariq removed the hood to reveal Noor's dark eyes, her spirit on fire. The falcon shivered and gave a series of quick, excited chirps before stretching her wings, ready to head for the sky and hunt.

Jayne could feel the beat of her wings against the air as she rose. Noor was swift and agile and her enjoyment was evident.

"Her eyesight is about eight times as sharp as yours or mine," Tariq said, as she hovered overhead when he moved the lure. The falcon's shadow passed over them and she climbed into the distance.

"She's gone."

"She's waiting." Tariq sounded very sure. "If I flush those pigeons out of that date palm, she'll appear."

He strode forward, waving his arms. The flock rose.

"Look."

Rocketing groundward, her wings folded back, Noor swooped down on an unsuspecting bird. No hesitation. Strike. And feathers exploded.

Tariq signalled and she tore into her meal. When the falcon had finished he waved the lure but Noor turned her back on him.

"See? A falconer needs endless patience. Noor is not yet ready to come home."

His generous mouth was curved into a smile. Jayne's heart skipped a beat as the memory of Tariq's patience as a lover swept her. She felt herself flush. She had to stop thinking about his lovemaking.

Noor rose into the air again, beating her wings. She climbed higher, a flash of the sun on her wings, and she disappeared into the blue.

Tariq pointed the antenna upward. The signal sounded. "She's over on the other side of that hedge. She must have taken another pigeon without us seeing. I'll give her a few more minutes and then we'll go collect her."

A few minutes later Noor hadn't moved.

"She's feasting," Tariq surmised.

But when they reached the other side of the hedge, there was no sign of Noor. A search revealed the transistor lying on the ground and a couple of floating feathers indicating a scuffle.

There was a white line around Tariq's mouth. "Noor is gone."

Foreboding filled Tariq as he and Jayne made their way back to the palace. He was aware that she kept sending him little concerned glances. But he didn't want her to see his eyes, in case she worked out what he was thinking.

The last time she had left Zayed, Khan had gone missing and had never returned.

Now it was Noor who was gone.

Tariq couldn't stop the gnawing fear that it was an omen that Jayne was about to leave. And when she did, he would never see her again.

They spent an hour driving around, searching for the falcon, to no avail. When they returned to the palace, an older woman stood in the hallway. A western woman. Tariq slowed at the sight of her. Her eyes were the colour of jade and her dark hair was drawn off her pale face and secured into a chic knot.

Her gaze locked with his. She stepped forward, then halted. She started to say something, but then she simply shook her head.

Beside him, Jayne gasped.

"You are my mother?" His words sounded rusty.

She nodded. Her eyes glistened with tears. She appeared to be incapable of speech.

"Welcome to Zayed," he said formally.

Jayne rushed into the sudden silence. "I'm Jayne, Tariq's wife."

"I am so pleased to meet you. You may call me Athina." As his mother hugged Jayne, Tariq could see that her hands were shaking.

Then Athina drew a deep breath and turned to him. "Thank you for calling me. Can you ever forgive me, my son? I wanted to take you with me, when you were a little boy, but I couldn't. You were your father's first-born child, his only child. His heir."

Tariq inclined his head stiffly. "I know you could not take me. In terms of the laws of Zayed, all children stay with the father when the woman leaves."

Jayne went white. Tariq realised that she must be thinking of her own child. If the child had been his, she would never have been allowed to leave Zayed until the child had been born.

Was it possible that she'd been carrying his child when she had left? Was it his child that she had lost?

Had his father lied? A bitter, sinking sensation roiled in the pit of his stomach. On top of everything else that was happening…his father's illness…his mother's arrival…Noor's disappearance…it was all too much to take in.

"I never loved your father," his mother was saying. "Then I met someone else." His mother must have seen something in his face, because she quickly added, "It was wrong what I did. When I fell pregnant I had to make a terrible choice."

"So you went." His voice was flat, empty of the hurt that her desertion had caused when he had been a child.

"I couldn't stay. If anyone had found out, I would've been sent to jail, my daughter taken away. I'm very grateful that you have invited me to Zayed to say goodbye to Rashid…and perhaps start over with you?"

"We can talk later," Tariq said. "I called you because my wife believes that my father needs to see you. Your gratitude should be to her." Jayne's hand slipped into his, and Tariq gripped it tightly.

Since their return from the desert, Jayne had avoided the Emir's bedchamber and Tariq had visited his father alone. But with the arrival of his mother, Tariq made it clear that he wanted her to come along, and Jayne had no choice but to accompany Tariq and Athina to see the Emir.

What would she have done if she'd been faced with the dilemma that Tariq's mother had?

A cold fist clutched Jayne's heart. Perhaps it was better that Tariq had never believed that the child she carried was his. She would never have been able to leave her child behind. Where would that have left her? Trapped in an existence where she stayed in Jazirah simply to be near the child she'd lost?

A shiver snaked down her spine. That would've been unbearable.

When they arrived at the Emir's chambers, the male nurse sprang to his feet. "His Excellency has been tired today."

"I know," Tariq said. "He said so earlier."

Jayne lurked in the background, letting Athina and Tariq go ahead. The Emir shifted against the pillows. "Lina?" He murmured. "I have been praying that you would come. I need your help."

Athina took the thin, bony hand. "What is it, Rashid?"

"It is our son."

"What is it, father?" Tariq moved to his father's bedside. "You need to relax, take it easy."

"Where is your wife? Where is Jayne?" The Emir lifted his head off the pillow, but the effort was too much and his head fell back. "I need to talk to her."

Jayne sensed that the Emir wanted—needed—to talk, a burning desire she did not share. It was far too late for talking. Years too late.

"Jayne, can you come closer?" he said.

She stood her ground. Did he regret what he had done? Did he want her forgiveness before he faced death? He'd taken her dreams and trampled on them, destroyed the love in her heart. She didn't know that she had space for forgiveness in the withered remains of what had once been a heart.

Jayne turned to face him. "I came back to Zayed to get a divorce."

"Jayne!" Tariq grabbed her arm.

She yanked it free. "No, I will not lie."

The Emir's face fell, his eyes grew distant and bleak. "I had hoped…" His voice grew weak.

For a terrible moment Jayne felt…ashamed. Then she told herself she had nothing to feel ashamed about. She had never done a thing to harm the Emir. But he had plotted to destroy her marriage to Tariq. He had caused her to run…to collapse…and he had caused her to—

God! She couldn't bear to think about the loss. The loss that she carried with her every day of her life.

She owed him nothing.

Nothing!

She hardened her gaze—and what was left of her heart.

Let him go to hell.

Let him know what it felt like.

She hoped he suffered. He deserved everything that was coming to him.

"Lina, this is why I need your help." The Emir's voice was thready. "I have done our son's wife an enormous wrong."

"What are you saying, Father?" Tariq asked urgently. "Tell me."

"What have you done, Rashid?"

Only Jayne said nothing, her eyes fixed on the frail old man in the high cot. A chill had seeped into her. She felt as if she would never be warm again.

"I told Tariq that she had committed adultery and slept with another man."

"It was untrue?" Tariq's cheekbones stood out under his skin. He looked suddenly haggard.

"What do you think, my son?"

Tariq looked wildly around at Jayne. "She told me she'd never been unfaithful. But I wouldn't believe her. Instead I believe you, my father." There was terrible pain in his voice. And Jayne saw the anguish in his eyes as full impact hit him. Tariq reached for her icy hand. "My child! Jayne, I'm sorry you were alone when you miscarried our child."

He believed the child belonged to him. But Jayne didn't feel relief or jubilation. She simply felt numb, and she stared at the Emir and waited.

"Tariq, Jayne didn't miscarry the child." The Emir broke off.

"What do you mean?" Emotion flared in Tariq's eyes. "My child is alive? Where?"

"I have a grandchild?" Lina sounded overjoyed.

The Emir shook his head slowly from side to side on the pillow. He was deathly pale. "It is my fault. When Jayne left, I gave her money to abort the baby. I didn't want your first-born son belonging to a woman I had not chosen for you."

"Father!" Tariq looked shattered. He turned to Jayne. "You told me all this, that my father drove you away, and I thought you were paranoid."

Athina's hands cupped her mouth. "Rashid, these are terrible things that you have done."

"I know." The sheikh stared at his hard-faced son. "I ask your forgiveness. Your mother asked many times to see you while you were growing up and I refused to grant her access. She tried to get visitation rights through the courts, I blocked her at every turn. I want to make things right before I die."

Nausea rose in Jayne's throat. She turned and slipped out of the room. Down the passage she entered a bedroom and made for the en suite bath. She clutched her stomach and waited for the nausea to pass.

"Are you all right?"

Tariq came up behind her and swung her around into his arms.

"Yes," Jayne said, standing stiffly in his hold. But she knew she wasn't. This could never be made right.

"You aborted our child?" Pain glowed in Tariq's eyes giving the gold the sheen of fire.

Jayne recoiled. "I—"

He tilted her chin up and stared down into her eyes. "You wrote me a miserable little missive advising me you had lost our baby. Lost, what does that mean?" The lack of expression in his voice made the demand more lethal. "Did you *miscarry* my child?"

Slowly Jayne shook her head.

"Allah, help me!" He threw his head back and the skin stretched taut across his facial bones. His fingers dug into her arms where he held her. "You aborted my son."

Jayne pulled out of his arms and crossed to lean against the marble slab of the basin. "The unborn baby that you wouldn't believe yours was a girl. A tiny, perfect little girl." Pain splintered inside her. Jayne was beyond tears. "I held her in my arms, I named her. And then I lost her."

"Lost? She was born alive? She died?"

Crossing her arms over her chest, Jayne hugged herself tightly. The cold refused to recede. "She is alive. I gave her up for adoption." It was the hardest thing she had ever said.

Tariq came toward her. "You took my daughter away from Zayed…away from me…and gave her to someone else?"

"Yes." The look Jayne gave him stopped him in his tracks. "I gave her to my sister. Helen can't have children. Samantha is adopted, and now she has Amy, as well." Her voice grew fierce. "And you cannot take Amy away from her mother. I won't allow it."

Tariq looked shaken by her ferocity. "But you are her *mother.*"

"No, I am not her mother. And you are not her father."

"Tariq! Jayne…come quickly."

At Athina's frantic calls they both hurried out of the bedroom.

"What is it?" Tariq demanded.

Athina's hand was over her mouth. "Rashid is…not well. You need to hurry."

Tariq started to run.

By the time Jayne got to the sick room, the Emir's breaths were coming in loud rasps.

"Slowly, Father," Tariq was saying. "The doctor will be here in a minute."

Jayne came up to the Emir's bedside. "I want you to know that my baby is alive. Her name is Amy. She is beautiful."

The old sheikh opened his eyes. They held a faraway glaze. "Thank you for that, Jayne, daughter. Now I have a chance of looking forward to paradise. Look after Amy. And look after my son—he needs you."

Unexpectedly a lump formed in her throat. Jayne knew that the divorce she had come to Zayed to finalise would never happen. How could she ever leave Tariq? "I will."

"Tariq?"

Tariq came up beside Jayne. "Yes, Father?"

"There is a parcel of land I want you to gift to Karim." He

gasped and coughed, a hacking sound. "It has leases made over to Ali—"

"I will take care of it, Father."

"And look after your—" he struggled for breath "—your mother."

"Yes," Tariq vowed. And tears pricked at the back of Jayne's throat when she saw the look he gave Athina. There was a long road for them to travel to get to know each other, but clearly Tariq was prepared to make a start.

"And keep your wife happy. Learn from my mistakes."

"Yes." But this time Tariq sounded less certain.

"Lina…?" The Emir's voice was panicky.

"I am here." Athina moved to the other side of the bed and took his hand. "I won't go."

"Thank you." There was a long pause, then he whispered, "I loved you. But I never told you how much. You thought it was all about the oil."

Athina shook her head. From across the bed, Jayne could feel the woman's shock. Jayne's gaze lifted to meet Tariq's and her breath caught at the naked emotion she read there.

Twelve

The funeral took place two days later.

Jayne couldn't believe the number of famous faces that attended. Statesmen and businessmen from all over Europe and the Gulf region were present. Karim al Bashir was there. Farrah Jirah had come to pay her respects and so had Ali and Mahood, along with a very subdued-looking Leila.

Tariq's Kyriakos cousins had flown in from Greece. Athina introduced Jayne to her nephews, Zac and Angelo and their wives Pandora and Gemma. Afterwards, back in the palace gardens where coffee and refreshments were served, Jayne found herself chatting to Pandora, Zac's wife, and his sister, Katy. There was a sense of sadness about Katy, and Jayne made a mental note to ask Tariq about it later.

Angelo's wife, Gemma, was beautiful, with clouds of dark-red hair. She glanced from Jayne to Tariq, and Jayne sensed her curiosity about their off-again, on-again marriage.

A sudden familiar chirp caused Jayne to turn her head. There, on a pole sat a familiar shape.

Noor!

She looked around for Tariq and saw that he'd already seen the falcon and was moving stealthily to the base of the pole. She could see his relief at her return from the intensity of his expression.

Tariq loved his falcons. But he expected no love back from the wild birds. His love was unconditional. He'd loved his father. But expected no love back—only pride.

Her husband had grown up in a hard world surrounded by men…no women to soften him. No women to love him.

Except her.

And she did love him.

Yet he had no idea how to respond to her love. Should she really be surprised?

It's easy to come to an understanding with a falcon. The falcon simply has to stay hungrier.

His words echoed in her head.

Loving Tariq was never going to be easy.

"Jayne."

She turned and scanned Tariq's features. He was holding up well under the strain, but she knew that the suddenness of his father's death had taken him by surprise—even though the doctor had said it was not unusual for cancer patients to have a short upswing, at times to feel a little better, before the end came.

"It's great that Noor is back."

"I'm taking her back to the mews. I've hardly seen you

over the last two days. When I come back, we need to make some time to talk."

Jayne looked at him in surprise. In the past Tariq had never worried about her, about making time to spend time together, much less talk. But he was right. They did need to talk.

"I want to see…her."

They sat in Tariq's study in front of his computer. On the screen was a photo of Amy on her first day at school. Jayne had no need to ask who Tariq was referring to. He couldn't take his eyes off the computer screen.

"Why?" she asked baldly. "What will it help to meet Amy? It will only unsettle you. Amy can never know who you are."

He rocked forward on the chair. "I want my daughter back. What you did—kidnapping her—was illegal. She should never have been taken from me, or out of Zayed."

Jayne shook her head and apprehension blossomed inside her as she stared at him. "It's too late, Tariq. You cannot take her away from the only family she has ever known."

"The adoption is illegal. She should never have left Zayed."

Dread turned Jayne's blood to ice. "How can you say that? You banished me. I tried to tell you that Amy was your baby, that I had never betrayed you. You wouldn't listen. You wanted me to prove my fidelity with a DNA test."

"I was a fool!"

"You're being a fool now, too. You can't have Amy back."

"I have to see her."

Now a very real fear fluttered in her stomach. "Promise me, Tariq, that you will not take her away from my sister."

He turned his gaze away from the screen. His eyes were dark-gold pools of anguish. *"I can't."*

Jayne raised her chin. "If you use your power and wealth to take her away from my sister, I will never forgive you."

The flight to Auckland was long but passed without incident. After they'd booked into a five-star hotel on the Princess Wharf, Jayne called Helen. After she set the phone down, she turned to Tariq, "We've been invited to tea tomorrow afternoon."

"Tea?" Tariq looked hunted. "How am I supposed to drink tea at a time like this?"

"You have no choice," she replied with a touch of sadness and wished, for a brief moment, that everything had been different.

The following day they climbed into the hire car and Tariq drove them to Remuera where Helen lived. They pulled up outside the neat, modern town house and opened the gate to the fenced yard where a swing hung from the branch of a giant oak in the corner of the property.

Tariq looked around with interest, wanting to assess if his daughter had been looked after…or neglected. But there was no evidence of neglect here.

The house shone with love and care. A row of pots filled with colour stood along the deck leading to the front door, and the windows were clean and shiny. The house looked happy— like it was smiling.

He shook off the fanciful thought and strode to the front door. Lifting the polished brass knocker, he rapped three times.

The front door opened. And his heart turned over. His daughter looked up at him. And Tariq fell in love. Completely and utterly.

Amy was the most beautiful human he had ever seen. She had pale skin with the lustre of a pearl—like Jayne's, with Jayne's sleek dark hair. But her eyes were gold and wild. His eyes.

"You are—" He broke off. How could he tell this beautiful child she was his daughter?

The daughter his father had paid her mother to abort.

God!

"Hello," he said instead.

"Who are you?" she asked, her gaze steady, not returning his greeting.

His throat tightened, he answered, "I am your—" *father* "—your Auntie Jayne's husband."

"Then it's okay to talk to you. My mummy doesn't allow me to talk to strangers."

Stranger.

His flesh and blood. His child. It hurt. Unbearably. Her mummy was not Jayne, her mummy was Jayne's sister. He pressed the heels of his palms against his eyes.

God!

"Is your head sore?" There was concern in the golden eyes. Definitely his eyes. "When my head gets sore I sometimes drink some water and it helps the dehyd—" She broke off and frowned.

He wanted to kiss the frown lines away.

"Dehydration," he supplied.

"Yes, that's what it helps."

Tariq knew that water wouldn't help his pain. His heart was breaking. If he claimed this beautiful child, flesh-of-his-flesh, he would lose Jayne. He had no doubt of that.

He'd spent too many years without his wife. He wanted her back.

But he looked at Amy. They should have been a family. He, Jayne and Amy. But his distrust had killed that.

What in hell had he done?

Jayne watched her husband sipping tea from her sister's favourite bone china and marvelled at his ability to hide his thoughts behind those hawklike eyes. Looking at him, no one would have realised what this occasion meant—except for the hypersensitivity he displayed to Amy's needs. It was after he'd indulged her for the third time by passing her the plate of Tim Tams that Helen murmured, "He knows she's his daughter."

Jayne simply nodded.

"Oh, Lord, please help us." Helen sprang up and hurried from the room.

Instantly concern lit Nigel's eyes, but before he could rise, Jayne gestured for him to stay and went searching for Helen.

She found Helen leaning against the fridge, her eyes stark with misery. "He's going to take her from us, isn't he?"

"Helen—"

"How can we fight him? He has wealth beyond everything we know." Helen sounded wild with grief.

"Helen—"

"I cannot take the child from her mother."

Both of them turned. Tariq stood in the doorway, Nigel's anxious face appeared behind him.

Tariq moved forward. "I have lost my daughter through my own actions, my own stupidity. You will not lose your daughter because of my shortsightedness."

"You don't want Amy?" Helen breathed.

"Of course I want Amy! But in the past hour, I have discovered she is no longer mine. She speaks of her sister

Samantha, her mother and father, her school friends. She has a life in which the most I can hope to be is a favourite uncle." He sighed. "I lost all claim to Amy years ago. My stupidity lost Jayne her daughter, too. I have to live with that every day of my life. But I am fortunate enough that I have not lost the wife I love more than anything in the world."

Jayne's breath caught at the anguish in his eyes. "You love me?"

"Of course, I do, *nuur il-en*. I nearly lost you, too."

She moved up beside him. "There will be other children."

"But never a first-born with your hair and my eyes. She is lost to us forever." The pain in his voice made her choke.

"Tariq…" Helen's hand closed on his shoulder. "You and Jayne are welcome to visit anytime you want. Perhaps when she's older she can go and stay with you during the holidays— if she wants."

"You are prepared to let her visit us? Halfway across the world?"

"Helen is saying more. She's going to tell Amy who her parents are. That's what you mean, isn't it?" Jayne raised an eyebrow at her sister.

Helen glanced at Nigel. He nodded.

"Yes," said Helen. "We will tell her."

Tariq put his arm around Jayne and pulled her close. "If Amy—or Samantha—ever need anything, you tell me, and they will get it. I am a blessed man."

Back in their hotel room overlooking the harbour, Jayne said, "Are you going to say it again?"

"Say what?" Tariq dropped down onto the enormous bed and lay back against the pillows.

"Are you going to tell me you love me again?"

Tariq's face grew grave. "I am going to pay attention to my father's advice. My mother didn't know he loved her, so she found someone else. I am going to treat you far better than I did the first time around. I will not neglect you, and I will make sure you know I love you. I am not risking losing you again. And that is a promise."

"I love you, too," she said. She fingered the amber and turquoise necklace she wore. "I don't need you to buy me ingots…or gold. All I wanted was your trust."

"You have it, Jayne." He frowned. "Are you going to be able to leave Auckland…and Amy?"

She drew a deep breath, "When we were in the desert, Matra said to me that in the desert one Bedouin will inquire another about grazing by asking, *Fih hayah*."

"It means 'Is there life?'" Tariq said, looking a little puzzled.

"I want you to know that you are my water. Without you my life is a desert and there is no life."

"My wife!" His eyes flared and the heat started to burn.

"I can live in Zayed, I have grown to have a better understanding of the desert. Farrah is keen for a literacy program to be set up for the rural women. I'd like to do it." She moved to sit next to him on the bed. "And I can register for the studies I want to do through London. And that's the easy stuff. The hard part is that I will miss Amy—I have always seen her regularly. That will be hard. It's going to feel like a piece is ripped out of me, not to have her nearby."

"I am sorry."

And he was. Jayne could read the torment in his eyes. "Don't be. She is beautiful. And she has made Helen and Nigel very happy. She has completed their family."

"You are too generous, *nuur il-en.*"

"I can afford to be," Jayne said, as she leaned forward to kiss the husband who looked so fierce but melted under her touch. "I've got you, my heart's desire."

* * * * *

Watch for Tessa Radley's next release
PRIDE & A PREGNANCY SECRET
part of the Diamonds Down Under *continuity*
Available February 2008
Only from Silhouette Desire.

Special Edition®

Life, Love and Family

*These contemporary romances will strike a chord
with you as heroines juggle life
and relationships on their way to true love.*

New York Times *bestselling author Linda Lael Miller
brings you a BRAND-NEW contemporary story
featuring her fan-favorite McKettrick family.*

Meg McKettrick is surprised to be reunited with her
high school flame, Brad O'Ballivan. After enjoying a
career as a country-and-western singer, Brad aches for
a home and family…and seeing Meg again makes him
realize he still loves her. But their pride manages to
interfere with love…until an unexpected matchmaker
gets involved.

*Turn the page for a sneak preview of
THE McKETTRICK WAY
by Linda Lael Miller
On sale November 20, wherever books are sold.*

Brad shoved the truck into gear and drove to the bottom of the hill, where the road forked. Turn left, and he'd be home in five minutes. Turn right, and he was headed for Indian Rock.

He had no damn business going to Indian Rock.

He had nothing to say to Meg McKettrick, and if he never set eyes on the woman again, it would be two weeks too soon.

He turned right.

He couldn't have said why.

He just drove straight to the Dixie Dog Drive-In.

Back in the day, he and Meg used to meet at the Dixie Dog, by tacit agreement, when either of them had been away. It had been some kind of universe thing, purely intuitive.

Passing familiar landmarks, Brad told himself he ought to turn around. The old days were gone. Things had ended badly between him and Meg anyhow, and she wasn't going to be at the Dixie Dog.

He kept driving.

He rounded a bend, and there was the Dixie Dog. Its big neon sign, a giant hot dog, was all lit up and going through its corny sequence—first it was covered in red squiggles of light, meant to suggest ketchup, and then yellow, for mustard.

Brad pulled into one of the slots next to a speaker, rolled down the truck window and ordered.

A girl roller-skated out with the order about five minutes later.

When she wheeled up to the driver's window, smiling, her eyes went wide with recognition, and she dropped the tray with a clatter.

Silently Brad swore. Damn if he hadn't forgotten he was a famous country singer.

The girl, a skinny thing wearing too much eye makeup, immediately started to cry. "I'm sorry!" she sobbed, squatting to gather up the mess.

"It's okay," Brad answered quietly, leaning to look down at her, catching a glimpse of her plastic name tag. "It's okay, Mandy. No harm done."

"I'll get you another dog and a shake right away, Mr. O'Ballivan!"

"Mandy?"

She stared up at him pitifully, sniffling. Thanks to the copious tears, most of the goop on her eyes had slid south. "Yes?"

"When you go back inside, could you not mention seeing me?"

"But you're Brad O'Ballivan!"

"Yeah," he answered, suppressing a sigh. "I know."

She rolled a little closer. "You wouldn't happen to have a picture you could autograph for me, would you?"

"Not with me," Brad answered.

"You could sign this napkin, though," Mandy said. "It's only got a little chocolate on the corner."

Brad took the paper napkin and her order pen, and scrawled his name. Handed both items back through the window.

She turned and whizzed back toward the side entrance to the Dixie Dog.

Brad waited, marveling that he hadn't considered incidents like this one before he'd decided to come back home. In retrospect, it seemed shortsighted, to say the least, but the truth was, he'd expected to be—Brad O'Ballivan.

Presently Mandy skated back out again, and this time she managed to hold on to the tray.

"I didn't tell a soul!" she whispered. "But Heather and Darlene *both* asked me why my mascara was all smeared." Efficiently she hooked the tray onto the bottom edge of the window.

Brad extended payment, but Mandy shook her head.

"The boss said it's on the house, since I dumped your first order on the ground."

He smiled. "Okay, then. Thanks."

Mandy retreated, and Brad was just reaching for the food when a bright red Blazer whipped into the space beside his. The driver's door sprang open, crashing into the metal speaker, and somebody got out in a hurry.

Something quickened inside Brad.

And in the next moment Meg McKettrick was standing practically on his running board, her blue eyes blazing.

Brad grinned. "I guess you're not over me after all," he said.

Silhouette®

SPECIAL EDITION™

**brings you a heartwarming
new McKettrick's story from**

NEW YORK TIMES BESTSELLING AUTHOR

LINDA LAEL MILLER

THE MCKETTRICK *Way*

Meg McKettrick is surprised to be reunited
with her high school flame, Brad O'Ballivan,
who has returned home to his family's
neighboring ranch. After seeing Meg again,
Brad realizes he still loves her. But the pride
of both manage to interfere with love...until
an unexpected matchmaker gets involved.

—— McKettrick Women ——

Available December wherever you buy books.

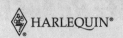

REQUEST YOUR FREE BOOKS!

2 FREE NOVELS PLUS 2 FREE GIFTS!

Passionate, Powerful, Provocative!

YES! Please send me 2 FREE Silhouette Desire® novels and my 2 FREE gifts. After receiving them, if I don't wish to receive any more books, I can return the shipping statement marked "cancel." If I don't cancel, I will receive 6 brand-new novels every month and be billed just $3.80 per book in the U.S., or $4.47 per book in Canada, plus 25¢ shipping and handling per book and applicable taxes, if any*. That's a savings of almost 15% off the cover price! I understand that accepting the 2 free books and gifts places me under no obligation to buy anything. I can always return a shipment and cancel at any time. Even if I never buy another book from Silhouette, the two free books and gifts are mine to keep forever.

225 SDN EEXJ 326 SDN EEXU

Name	(PLEASE PRINT)	
Address		Apt.
City	State/Prov.	Zip/Postal Code

Signature (if under 18, a parent or guardian must sign)

Mail to the **Silhouette Reader Service™**:
IN U.S.A.: P.O. Box 1867, Buffalo, NY 14240-1867
IN CANADA: P.O. Box 609, Fort Erie, Ontario L2A 5X3

Not valid to current Silhouette Desire subscribers.

Want to try two free books from another line?
Call 1-800-873-8635 or visit www.morefreebooks.com.

* Terms and prices subject to change without notice. NY residents add applicable sales tax. Canadian residents will be charged applicable provincial taxes and GST. This offer is limited to one order per household. All orders subject to approval. Credit or debit balances in a customer's account(s) may be offset by any other outstanding balance owed by or to the customer. Please allow 4 to 6 weeks for delivery.

Your Privacy: Silhouette is committed to protecting your privacy. Our Privacy Policy is available online at www.eHarlequin.com or upon request from the Reader Service. From time to time we make our lists of customers available to reputable firms who may have a product or service of interest to you. If you would prefer we not share your name and address, please check here. ☐

SDES07

ATHENA FORCE

Heart-pounding romance and thrilling adventure.

She's their ace in the hole.

Posing as a glamorous high roller, Bethany James, a
professional gambler and sometimes government agent,
uncovers a mob boss's deadly secrets…and the ugly sins
from his past. But when a daredevil with a tantalizing
drawl calls her bluff, the stakes—and her heart rate—
become much, much higher. Beth can't help but wonder:
Have the cards been finally stacked against her?

ATHENA FORCE

Will the women of Athena unravel Arachne's
powerful web of blackmail and death…or succumb
to their enemies' deadly secrets?

Look for

STACKED DECK
by *Terry Watkins*.

Introducing

a brand-new miniseries with light-hearted and playful stories that will make you Blush... because who says that sex has to be serious?

Starting in December with...

BABY, IT'S COLD OUTSIDE
by Cathy Yardley

Chilly temperatures send Colin Reeves and Emily Stanfield indoors—then it's sparks, sensual heat and hot times ahead! But will their private holiday hometown reunion last longer than forty-eight delicious hours in bed?

COMING NEXT MONTH

#1837 THE EXECUTIVE'S SURPRISE BABY—
Catherine Mann
The Garrisons
The news of his impending fatherhood was shocking…
discovering the mother of his baby didn't want to marry him—
unbelievable.

#1838 SPENCER'S FORBIDDEN PASSION—
Brenda Jackson
A Westmoreland bachelor got more than he bargained for when
he turned his hostile takeover bid into a marriage-of-convenience
offer.

#1839 RICH MAN'S VENGEFUL SEDUCTION—
Laura Wright
No Ring Required
He had one goal: seduce the woman who left him years ago and
leave her cold. Could he carry out his plan after a night together
ignites old passions?

#1840 MARRIED OR NOT?—Annette Broadrick
The last person she needed or wanted to see was her
ex-husband…until she discovered they could still be man and
wife.

#1841 HIS STYLE OF SEDUCTION—Roxanne St. Claire
She was charged with giving this millionaire a makeover. But she
was the one in for a big change...in the bedroom.

#1842 THE MAGNATE'S MARRIAGE DEMAND—
Robyn Grady
A wealthy tycoon demanded the woman pregnant with the heir
to his family dynasty marry him. But their passionate union was
anything but all business.

SDCNM1107